"We must marry."

Shock held Gina rigid for several seconds, her mind blank of all rational thought. "That's quite ridiculous!" she managed at length.

"It is the only way I have of restoring honor."

"Because of last night? But it was my own choice."

"It makes no difference. It is my duty to make reparation."

Lucius was speaking with a clipped quietness more telling than any amount of ranting and raving. "Arrangements will be made immediately."

Kay Thorpe

THE ITALIAN MATCH

ITALIAN
HUSBANDS

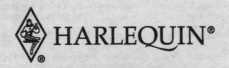

HARLEQUIN®

TORONTO • NEW YORK • LONDON
AMSTERDAM • PARIS • SYDNEY • HAMBURG
STOCKHOLM • ATHENS • TOKYO • MILAN • MADRID
PRAGUE • WARSAW • BUDAPEST • AUCKLAND

ISBN 0-373-12312-4

THE ITALIAN MATCH

First North American Publication 2003.

Copyright © 2001 by Kay Thorpe.

This edition published by arrangement with Harlequin Books S.A.

Visit us at www.eHarlequin.com

Printed in U.S.A.

CHAPTER ONE

STRANGE to think that this could have been her homeland, Gina reflected, viewing the lush Tuscany landscape spread before her as the car breasted the rise. Beautiful as it was, she felt no particular draw to the place.

Pulling into the roadside, she took a look at the map laid open across the passenger seat. If her calculations were correct, the collection of red-slate roofs and single-bell tower some mile or so distant had to be Vernici. Smaller than she had imagined, though big enough to offer some kind of accommodation for the short time she was likely to be spending in the vicinity. This close to her destination, she still had doubts as to the wisdom of what she was planning to do. Twenty-five years was a long time. It could be that the Carandentes no longer even resided in the area.

If that turned out to be the case, she would put the whole thing behind her once and for all, she vowed. If nothing else, she would have seen parts of Europe she had never seen before.

Surrounded by olive groves, the little town had an almost medieval air about it, its narrow streets radiating from a central piazza. The car that burst from one of the narrow streets at breakneck speed would have hit Gina's car head-on if she hadn't taken instant evading action. There was only one way to go, and that was straight through a flimsy barrier protecting some kind of road works, finishing up tilted at a crazy angle with her offside front wheel firmly lodged in the deep hole.

Held by the safety belt, she had suffered no more than a severe shaking up, but the shock alone was enough to keep her sitting there like a dummy for the few moments it took people attracted by the screeching of brakes to put in an appearance.

Her scanty Italian could make neither head nor tail of the voluble comment. All she could do was make helpless gestures. Eventually one man got the passenger door open and helped her clamber out of the vehicle, all the time attempting to make himself understood.

The only word Gina recognised was garage. *'Si, grazie, signor!'* she responded thankfully, trusting to luck that he would take her meaning and call someone out for her. That the car would be in no fit state to be driven when it was pulled out of the hole, she didn't doubt. She simply had to hope that repairs could be effected without too much trouble.

Her helpmate disappeared up a side street, leaving her to lean weakly against the nearest support and wait for succour. It was gone two, the heat scarcely diminished from its midday high; her sleeveless cotton blouse was sticking to her back. An elderly woman addressed her in tones of sympathy. Assuming that she was being asked if she was feeling all right. Gina conjured a smile and another *'Si, grazie. Inglese,'* she tagged on before any further questions could be put to her.

It might have been an idea to learn at least enough of the language to get by on before setting out on this quest of hers, she thought wryly, but it was a little late for if onlys. She was in Vernici, and quite likely going to be stuck here for however long it might take to get her car back on the road.

Straightening, she walked round the vehicle to view the uptilted front end, in no way reassured by what she saw.

The wheel had been crushed inwards by the impact, the whole wing and a corner of the bonnet badly crumpled. It was some small consolation that the car itself was Italian. If new parts were needed that surely had to help.

Hindered more than aided by the all-too-ready helping hands and eager advice, it took the two men who eventually arrived in a battered tow truck almost half an hour to drag the car free. It was, Gina saw with sinking heart, in an even worse state of disrepair than she had thought. The wheel was buckled, the wing a total write-off, the bonnet probably salvageable but unlikely to look pristine again without a lot of expert hammering and filling.

The happy-go-lucky manner employed by both mechanics gave little rise to confidence. One of them, who spoke some English, indicated that it would be necessary to send to Siena, or perhaps even to Florence for a new wheel and wing. When asked how long that might take, he spread his hands in a gesture only too easily recognisable. Perhaps a week, perhaps even longer. Who could tell? And then, of course, there would be the work. Perhaps another week. The possible cost? Once more the hands were spread. The cost would be what the cost would be, Gina gathered, by then in no fit state to press the issue any further.

Declining an offer to squeeze her into a seat between the two of them, she followed the truck on foot to a small backstreet garage, to see her only means of transport tucked away in a corner to await attention. The parts would be ordered at once, the younger man assured her. In the meantime, he could supply a good place for her to stay.

Faced with his overt appraisement of her body, Gina gave the suggestion scant consideration. For the first time she turned her mind to the car that had caused the accident. The driver had been female not male, and young, the car itself big and blue.

With faint hope, she described both car and occupant to her mechanic friend, to be rewarded with a grinning acknowledgement. 'Cotone,' he said. 'You go to San Cotone. Three kilometres,' he added helpfully, and drew a map in the dust. 'Very rich. You make them pay!'

Gina had every intention of trying. She was covered by insurance, of course, but claims for accidents abroad were notoriously difficult to get settled. The more she thought about it the angrier she became, her object in coming to Vernici in the first place temporarily pushed to the back of her mind. She was stuck out here in the back of beyond because of some spoiled teenager with nothing better to do than tear around the roads without regard for life or limb. Recklessness didn't even begin to cover it!

The question was how to reach the place. 'Taxi?' she queried. 'Bus?'

He shook his head. 'You take car.'

'How the devil can I—?' she began, breaking off abruptly when she saw where he was pointing. With almost as much rust as paint on the bodywork, and tyres that looked distinctly worn, the little Fiat's better days were obviously a long way in the past. Beggars, however, couldn't afford to be choosers. If that was the only vehicle available that was the one she would take.

'How much?' she asked.

The shrug was eloquent, the smile even more so. 'You pay later.'

In cash, not kind, she thought drily, reading him only too well. Her bags were locked in the boot of her own car. After a momentary hesitation she decided they would have to stay there for the present. She had to get this other matter settled while the anger still burned good and bright. The question of accommodation could wait.

Despite its appearance, the Fiat started without too much

trouble. Gina headed out along the route by which she had approached the town, to take the turning her adviser's drawing had indicated through the gently rolling landscape.

Olive groves gave way to immense vineyards tended by what appeared to be a regular army of workers. Only then did Gina make the connection with the label she had seen on Chianti wines back home. A rich family indeed, she thought, well able to pay for the damage to her car, for certain.

A pair of wide wrought-iron gates gave open access to a drive that curved through trees to reach a stone-built villa of stunning size and architecture. Gina drew to a stop on the gravelled circle fronting the place, refusing to allow the grandeur to deflect her from her aim. A member of this household had driven her off the road; the onus was on them to reimburse her.

Set into the stone wall beside imposing double doors, the bell was of the old-fashioned pull-type. It emitted a deep, repeated note, clearly audible from where she stood. The elderly man who answered the summons was dressed in dark trousers and matching waistcoat along with a sparkling white shirt. A member of staff rather than family, Gina judged. His appraisement was rapid, taking in her simple cotton skirt and blouse. The disdain increased as his glance went beyond her to the battered vehicle standing on the gravelled forecourt.

'I'm here to see the owner,' she stated before he could speak, wishing she had thought to get a name from her mechanic friend. *'Padrone,'* she tagged on, dredging the depths of her scanty vocabulary.

The man shook his head emphatically, loosed a single, terse sentence, and began to close the door again. Gina stopped the movement by placing her hands flat against the wood and shoving.

'*Padrone!*' she insisted.

From the look on the man's face, she wasn't getting through. Which left her with only one choice. She slipped past him before he could make any further move, heading for one of the doors leading off the wide, marble-floored hall with no clear idea in mind other than to block any immediate attempt to remove her from the premises.

There was a key in the far side lock. She slammed the heavy dark-wood door to and secured it, leaning her forehead against a panel to regain both her breath and her wits. That had been a really crazy thing to do, she admitted. A move hardly likely to impress the owner of the establishment, whoever he or she was.

A knock on the door was followed by what sounded like a question. Gina froze where she stood as another male voice answered, this time from behind her. She spun round, gaining a hazy impression of a large, book-lined room as her gaze came to rest on the man seated at a vast desk on the far side of it.

Slanting through the window behind him, the sun picked out highlights in the thick sweep of black hair. Dark eyes viewed her from beneath quizzically raised brows, the lack of anger or even annoyance on his leanly sculptured features something of a reassurance.

'*Buon pomeriggeo,*' he said.

'*Parla inglese?*' Gina asked hopefully.

'Of course,' he answered in fluent English. 'I apologise for my lack of perception. I was deceived by the blackness of your hair into believing you of the same blood as myself for a moment, but no Italian woman I ever met had so vividly blue a pair of eyes, so wonderfully fair a skin!'

A fairness that right now was more of a curse than an

asset, Gina could have told him, dismayed to feel warmth rising in her cheeks at the sheer extravagance of the observation. She was unaccustomed to such flowery language from a man. But then, how many Latins had she actually met before this?

'It should be me apologising for breaking in on you like this,' she said, taking a firm grip on herself, 'but it was the only way to get past the door guard.'

A smile touched the strongly carved mouth. 'As Guido speaks little English, whilst you obviously speak even less Italian, misunderstandings were certain to arise. Perhaps you might explain to me what it is that you are here for?'

Feeling like a stag at bay with her back braced against the door, Gina eased herself away, conscious of a sudden frisson down her spine as the man rose from his seat. No more than the early thirties, he had a lithe, athletic build beneath the cream silk shirt and deeper-toned trousers. Rolled shirt sleeves revealed muscular forearms, while the casually opened collar laid the strong brown column of his throat open to inspection.

'I need to see the head of the household,' she said, blanking out the involuntary response.

He inclined his head. 'I am Lucius Carandente.'

Shock robbed her of both speech and clarity of thought for a moment or two. She gazed at him with widened eyes. There had to be more than one Carandente family, she told herself confusedly. This couldn't possibly be them!

Yet why not? asked another part of her mind. She knew nothing of the family other than the name. Why assume it more likely that they be of proletarian rather than patrician stock?

The dark brows lifted again, a certain amused speculation in his gaze. 'You appear surprised.'

Gina pulled herself together. 'I was expecting someone

older,' she prevaricated, in no way ready to plumb any further depths as yet. 'The father, perhaps, of a girl who drives a blue tourer.'

Speculation gave way to sudden comprehension, all trace of amusement vanished. 'Donata,' he said flatly. 'My younger sister. What did she do?'

'She caused me to crash my car an hour or so ago. Down in Vernici. It's going to need new parts. The garage down there tells me they'll have to be ordered from Florence, and it's going to take a lot of time—to say nothing of the cost!'

'You carry no insurance?'

'Of course I carry insurance!' she returned with asperity, sensing an attempt to wriggle off the hook. 'Waiting for the go-ahead from my company would take even more time. In any case, it's your sister's insurance that should be responsible for the damage—always providing *she* carries some!'

She paused there, seeing his lips take on a slightly thinner line and aware of allowing her tongue to run away with her. 'I'm sorry,' she tagged on impulsively. 'That was very rude of me.'

'Yes, it was,' he agreed. 'Though perhaps not entirely unmerited. If you will kindly unlock the door behind you and allow Guido entrance, I will take the necessary steps.'

Gina obeyed with some faint reluctance, not at all certain that he wouldn't order Guido to toss her out on her ear. The manservant entered the room without haste, his glance going directly to his master as if she didn't even exist.

Lucius Carandente spoke in rapid Italian, despatching the older man with a final *'Subito!'*

'Please take a seat,' he told Gina, indicating the nearest of the deep club chairs.

He didn't sit down himself, but leaned against the desk edge as she complied, placing her at a distinct and probably intentional disadvantage. No matter, she thought resolutely; she could always stand up again if she felt the need.

'You have yet to give me your name,' he said.

'I'm sorry,' she proffered once more. 'I'm Gina Redman.'

'You are here on vacation?'

It was easier at the moment to say yes, Gina decided, not yet convinced that the name wasn't just a coincidence. Other than the obvious characteristics, this man bore no great resemblance to the photograph in her handbag.

'I'm touring,' she acknowledged. 'I've driven all the way through France and Switzerland without a single mishap. If your sister hadn't been going so fast...'

Lucius held up a hand. 'It would be better that we wait until she is available to speak for herself, I think. She arrived home, I know, so it should not be long before she joins us. Until then,' he added in the same courteous tones, 'we will talk of other matters. The colour of your hair does not suggest the English rose. Is it possible, perhaps, that you have mixed parentage?'

Short of telling him to mind his own business, Gina was left with no choice but to answer. 'My father was Italian.'

'Was?'

'He died before I was born.' She forestalled the next question, hoping he would leave it at that until she had time to consider just how she was going to find out if he was indeed one of the Carandentes she had come so far to find. 'I was adopted by my English stepfather.'

'I see.'

To her relief he refrained from asking the name discarded for Redman. He probably assumed that her mother had never held title to it to start with.

The opening of the door heralded the entry of a girl whose appearance was totally at odds with her surroundings. Multilayered and finger-raked into a rough tumble about her tempestuous young face, her hair looked more like a bird's nest than the crowning glory it must once have been. She was clad in black leather, the trousers skintight about rounded hips, the jacket outlining a well-endowed figure.

It was apparent at once that she recognised Gina, though she gave no sign of discomfiture. She addressed her brother in Italian, switching to English with no more effort than he had displayed himself when told to do so—and with even greater fluency.

'The blame wasn't mine,' she declared flatly, without glancing in Gina's direction. 'There's no damage to *my* car.'

'Only because I managed to avoid what would have been a head-on crash!' Gina asserted before Lucius could respond. 'You were going too fast to stop. You didn't even attempt to stop! Even to see if I was all right!' She was sitting bolt upright in the chair, not about to let the girl get away with her denials. 'Leaving the scene of an accident is against the law where I come from—especially where there are possible injuries to either party.'

'If you'd been injured you wouldn't be sitting here,' Donata returned.

Gina kept a tight rein on her temper. 'That's not the point. I'm going to be stuck in Vernici until my car can be repaired—with a hefty bill at the end of it. At the very least, I need your insurance details to pass on to mine.'

'But what you really want is for Lucius to give you money now!' flashed the younger girl.

Her brother said something short and sharp in Italian, increasing the mutinous set of her jaw. When she spoke again it was with sullen intonation. 'I'm sorry.'

Lucius made no attempt to stop her from leaving the room. His mouth tautened as the door slammed in her wake.

'I add my apologies for the way Donata spoke to you,' he said. 'I also apologise for her appearance. She returned last week from her school in Switzerland...' He broke off, shaking his head as if in acknowledgement that whatever he had been about to say was irrelevant to the present matter. 'I believe it best that I take responsibility for the financial affairs,' he said instead. 'You have accommodation already arranged?'

Gina shook her head, the wind taken completely out of her sails.

'So where is your luggage?'

'I left it locked in the boot of the car,' she said. 'My car, not the one I came here in. I hired that from the garage.'

'It will be returned, and your luggage brought here. If you give me your car keys I will make the necessary arrangements.'

'Here?' Gina looked at him in some confusion. 'I don't—'

'You will naturally stay at Cotone until your car is repaired,' he stated. 'That will be done in Siena.'

'I can't let you...' she began again, voice petering out as he lifted a staying hand.

'You must allow me to make what reparation I can for my sister's lack of care. It would be most discourteous of you to reject my hospitality.'

'Then I must of course accept,' she said after a moment. 'Thank you, *signor*.'

His smile sent a further quiver down her spine. 'You will please call me Lucius. And I may address you by your first name?'

'Of course,' she said, bemused by the totally unexpected turn of events. 'You're very kind.'

The dark eyes roved the face upturned to him, coming to rest on the curve of her mouth. 'I find it difficult to be otherwise with a beautiful woman. A weakness, I know.'

Gina gave a laugh, doing her best to ignore the curling stomach muscles. 'I doubt you'd allow anyone, male *or* female, to get the better of you!'

'I said difficult, not impossible,' came the smooth return.

His gaze shifted from her as the door opened again to admit a young maidservant. He must, Gina surmised, have summoned her via some hidden bell press.

'Crispina will show you to your room,' he said, having spoken to the girl. 'Your bags will be brought to you. Until then, you would be advised to rest. An ordeal such as the one you experienced can produce delayed shock.'

Gina didn't doubt it; she felt in the grip of it right now. She got to her feet, vitally aware of his eyes following her as she crossed to the door. Crispina answered her greeting smile with a somewhat tentative one of her own. She shook her head when Gina asked if she spoke English, which left the pair of them with very little to say as they climbed the grand staircase to the upper storey.

The bedroom to which she was shown was every bit as grand as the rest of the house, with glass doors opening onto a balcony that overlooked the magnificent view. The spacious *en suite* bathroom had fittings Gina was pretty sure were solid gold, the walls lined in mirror glass. She eyed her multireflection in wry acknowledgement of a less than pristine appearance. Clambering from a car halfway down a hole in the ground had left its mark in more ways then the one.

Back in the bedroom, she extracted the long envelope from her bag, and sat down on the bed edge to study the photograph afresh. Arms about each other, the young couple portrayed looked so blissfully happy, the girl's fair skin and pale gold hair a total contrast to her partner's Latin looks—both of them scarcely out of their teen years.

Gina had come across the photograph while browsing in the attic one rainy afternoon when she was fifteen. The accompanying marriage licence had tilted her world on its axis, the explanations reluctantly furnished by her mother when confronted with the evidence even more so.

Her mother and Giovanni Carandente had met as students at Oxford and had fallen madly in love. Knowing neither family would approve the match, they had married in secret, planning on taking their degrees before telling them. Her pregnancy had changed everything. Giovanni had set out to face his family with the news in person, only to meet his death in a road accident on the way to the airport. Two months later, with her parents still unaware of the truth, Beth had married her former boyfriend, John Redman, the two of them allowing everyone to believe that the baby was his.

Sitting here now, Gina went over the scene in her mind once again, recalling the anguish. Although she bore no facial resemblance, John Redman's colouring had always lent credence to hers. She would never in a thousand years have suspected the truth.

Asked why she hadn't attempted to contact the Carandentes herself, her mother had made a wry gesture. She knew nothing about them, she admitted, except that they lived in the town of Vernici in Tuscany. They had been the ones informed of Giovanni's death not her. She had found out only on reading about the accident in the following day's newspaper.

'It was a terrible time,' she acknowledged. 'I hardly knew which way to turn. If it hadn't been for your father—'

'But he isn't my father, is he?' Gina said hollowly.

'In every other way he is. He gave you his name—provided us both with a home and a good life. He's a good man. The very best.' Beth's voice was tender. 'I love him dearly.'

'But not the way you loved Giovanni?'

Beth shook her head, her smile wry again. 'No two loves are the same, darling. What Giovanni and I had was wonderful, but whether it would have lasted—well, who can tell?' She hesitated before continuing. 'I know it's a lot to ask, but can we keep it just between ourselves? John regards you as his own child. He'd be terribly upset if he knew that you knew you weren't.'

Loving him the way she did herself, she'd had no inclination to tell him what she knew, either then or since, Gina reflected, but the knowledge couldn't be wiped out. For years she had toyed with the idea of some day coming out here and searching for her forebears, only an idea was all it had been until now. She had three more weeks before she started the new job she hoped would rekindle the interest and ambition so lacking this last year or so. Once into that, her free time would be severely restricted.

It was coming up to six o'clock, she saw, glancing at her watch. She'd been sitting here for more than half an hour thinking about it all. The question of whether these Carandentes were of the same family line as her father still remained to be answered. The most direct way was to ask outright, of course, but she was somehow reluctant to do that.

A knock on the door signalled the arrival of her bags. Dinner, she was advised by Guido in fragmentary English, would be served at nine-thirty in the salon. The master requested that she join the family for prior refreshment on the terrace at nine.

Gina thanked the man, receiving a bare nod by way of return. It was obvious that her presence was not looked on with favour. As an old family retainer, he would naturally take Donata Carandente's side in the matter of who was to blame for the accident, she supposed. It was possible that the rest of the staff would take the same attitude— although Crispina had shown no sign of it.

Whether through the delayed shock Lucius had spoken of, or simply the effects of a long day behind the wheel, the weariness overtaking her was not to be denied. It was doubtful if she'd sleep, but a couple of hours just resting would revive her for the evening to come. She would hate to nod off over the dinner table.

She took off her outer clothing before lying down on the silk bedspread, stretching out luxuriously beneath the spinning fan. So much nicer than functional air-conditioning, she thought, watching the moving blades. The soft, whirring sound was soporific in itself.

Lucius had said Donata was his younger sister. Were there other siblings? For him to be *padrone*, his father must be dead too, but perhaps there was still a mother alive. If these people really did turn out to be her father's kith and kin, then she and Lucius could be cousins. She found the idea oddly displeasing.

Daylight had faded to a dim glimmer when she awoke. It was a relief to see there was still half an hour to go before she was expected to join the family on the terrace.

The sleep had refreshed her, the shower did an even

better job, but no amount of revitalisation could make what was to come any easier. At some point this evening she had to bring up her father's name and learn the truth. For peace of mind alone she needed to know her origins.

Having planned on staying at good hotels throughout her journey, she had packed clothes to suit most circumstances. Cut on the bias in deep blue silk jersey, the dress she picked out to wear to dinner skimmed her figure to finish on the knee. Teamed with a pair of high-heeled sandals, it should fit the bill, Gina reckoned.

A stroke or two of mascara along her lashes, a dash of lipstick, and she was ready to go. There hadn't been time to put her hair up into the French pleat she would have preferred, but it would have to do. Thick and glossy, it fell in soft waves to her shoulders—the bane of her life when it came to drying after washing, but she could never bring herself to have it cut short.

Night was fast encroaching when she reached the wide, stone-balustered terrace, the lamps already lit. Of the five people gathered there, three were female, the family resemblance pronounced.

Lucius came forward to greet her as she hesitated on the threshold of the room through which she had emerged, the look in his eyes as he scanned her shapely length tensing muscle and sinew. He was making no secret of the fact that he found her as much of a draw as she had to admit she found him. A man who might well be her cousin, she reminded herself forcibly. A first cousin, even.

The prospect of a family relationship was hardly enhanced by Donata's open hostility. Her sister, Ottavia, was around twenty-seven or eight and married to a man some few years older named Marcello Brizzi. Their response to the introduction was courteous enough on the surface, but it was apparent that they too regarded her presence as an intrusion.

It was left to the matriarch of the family to show any warmth in her welcome. Skin almost as smooth as Gina's own, the still luxuriant hair untouched by grey, she scarcely looked old enough to have a son Lucius's age.

'My son tells me you are half Italian yourself,' she said. 'I believe you never knew your father?'

Seated in one of the comfortable lounging chairs, the gin and tonic she had asked for to hand, Gina shook her head. 'He died before I was born.'

Signora Carandente expressed her sympathy in a long, drawn sigh. 'Such a terrible thing!' She was silent for a moment, contemplating the girl before her. 'You have older siblings, perhaps?'

Gina shook her head again, eliciting another sigh.

'For a man to die without a son to carry on his name is a sad matter indeed! Should anything happen to Lucius before he produces a son, our own lineage will be finished too. You would think, would you not, that he would recognise such a responsibility?'

'I am not about to die,' he declared calmly.

'Who can tell?' his mother returned. 'You must marry soon. You have a duty. And who better than Livia Marucchi!'

His shrug made light of the moment, but Gina sensed an underlying displeasure that such matters should be discussed in the presence of a stranger. She'd found the episode discomfiting enough herself. From what little she had seen of him, she judged him a man who would make his own decision about whom and when he should marry anyway. His choices, she was sure, would in no way be limited to one woman.

'What was your father's name?' asked Ottavia, jerking

her out of her thoughts and into sudden flaring panic. She wasn't ready! Not yet!

'Barsini,' she said, plucking the name out of some distant memory without pause for consideration. 'Alexander Barsini.'

She regretted the impulse the moment the words left her lips, but it was too late to retract.

'Barsini,' Ottavia repeated. 'Which part of Italy did he come from?'

Having begun it, she was left with no option but to continue, Gina acknowledged ruefully. 'Naples,' she said off the top of her head.

'He has family still living?'

This time Gina opted for at least a partial truth. 'I don't know. I came to Italy to try and find out.'

Ottavia's brows lifted in a manner reminiscent of her brother, though minus any humour. 'Your mother failed to maintain contact?'

Gina returned her gaze with a steadiness she was far from feeling. 'My mother never met his family. They knew nothing of the marriage.'

'I think that enough,' Lucius cut in before his sister could continue the catechism. 'Let the matter rest.'

Ottavia looked as if she found the command unpalatable, but she made no demur. Gina doubted, however, that her curiosity would remain contained. Catching Donata's eye, she tried a smile, receiving a glare in return. There would be no softening of attitude there for certain. She was well and truly in the doghouse!

Dinner proved less of a banquet than anticipated, with no more than four courses. Gina drank sparingly of the free-flowing wines. She loved the reds, but they didn't always love her. The last thing she needed was to waken with a hangover in the morning.

Lucius insisted that all conversation was conducted in English for her sake, which made her feel even more of an outsider. Marcello, she learned, was the estate comptroller, Ottavia a lady of leisure. The latter confined her questions this time to Gina's present background, expressing astonishment on hearing she was a qualified accountant.

'Such an unusual job for a woman!' she exclaimed. 'Do you not think so, Lucius?'

'An admirable achievement for anyone,' he returned, directing a smile that set every nerve in Gina's body tingling. 'Especially at so young an age.'

'I'm twenty-five,' she felt moved to respond. 'Not that much younger than yourself, I imagine.'

The smile came again, accompanied by an unmistakable glint in the dark eyes. 'Eight years is no obstacle, I agree.'

Obstacle to what, Gina didn't need to ask. Neither, she was sure, did anyone else. That his interest in her was purely physical she didn't need telling either. It could hardly be anything more.

Her cool regard served only to increase the glint. Opposition, it appeared, was an enticement in itself. More than ever she regretted the situation she had landed herself with. If she wanted to know the truth, not only was she faced with the prospect of explaining a lie she had no logical reason to have told in the first place, but the possibility of mortifying Lucius with the news that he had been making advances to a relative.

'And what does your stepfather do for a living?' Ottavia persisted, claiming her attention once more.

'He's in textiles,' she acknowledged.

'On his own account?'

'His own business, yes.' A highly successful one, Gina could have added, but saw no reason to go into greater detail—especially when said success was dependent on factors she found rather worrying at times.

Ottavia seemed content to leave it at that for the moment, but Gina sensed that the digging was by no means done. Plain nosiness, she assured herself. There was no way the woman could suspect the truth.

Midnight brought no sign of an end to the evening. Hardly able to keep her eyes open, Gina finally gave in.

'I hope it won't be taken amiss if I go to bed,' she said. 'I was on the road at seven this morning, and didn't have all that good a night's sleep before it.'

'But of course!' Signora Carandente responded. 'You must feel free to do whatever you wish while you are our guest. Perhaps you would prefer to have breakfast served in your room?'

'Not at all,' Gina assured her. 'I'll be fine.' She added impulsively, 'Your hospitality is second to none, *signora*.'

'Contessa,' corrected Ottavia with some sharpness of tone.

'You may call me Cornelia,' her mother told Gina graciously.

Still grappling with the implications, Gina inclined her head. 'Thank you.'

She took her leave with a general 'Goodnight,' avoiding any clash of glances with Lucius himself. If his mother was a Contessa, his father obviously had to have been a Count, which meant the title must have been handed down. It made the likelihood of her father having any connection seem even more remote. What would a son of such a family have been doing attending an English university as an ordinary student?

On the other hand, it was surely unlikely that either now or in the past another, entirely unconnected, Carandente family resided in Vernici.

She was going around in circles, Gina acknowledged. The only way to be sure was to do what she should have done several hours ago and tell the whole story. Concealing the name had been an idiotic gesture all round. Tomorrow, she promised herself, she would come clean. It was hardly as if she was after feathering her nest in any fashion. All she wanted was to know who her father had really been.

CHAPTER TWO

DESPITE her tiredness, Gina was wide awake at six. The early morning sunlight beckoned her out onto the balcony to view the beautifully landscaped gardens stretching to all sides. The vistas beyond were shrouded in early morning haze.

There was no one about that she could see from here. On impulse, she returned to the bedroom to don a pair of light cotton trousers and a shirt. Half an hour or so's exploration would still leave her plenty of time to get ready for the day proper.

She could hear the muted sound of voices coming from somewhere towards the rear of the premises as she descended to the lower floor, but no one appeared to question her purpose. Not that any member of staff would do that in any case, Gina supposed. As a guest of the house she was, as Cornelia had assured her, entitled to do as she wished.

All the same she reduced the chances of running into anyone by using the front entrance. The Fiat was gone, the driveway clear of vehicles of any kind. There would be garages around the back somewhere, she assumed.

She headed left, away from the house, dropping down stone steps between white marble pillars to terraces overhung with luxuriant plant life and strewn with classical statues. Gina revelled in the beauty of it all against the clean, clear blue of the sky.

On one level lay a pond laced with water lilies of every hue, the carved stone bench at its edge positioned to take full advantage of the harmonious view across the valley. She slowed her steps on sight of the man already seated there.

'I didn't realise anyone else was up and about yet,' she said a little awkwardly. 'I thought I'd take a look around before breakfast.'

'I saw you from my window,' Lucius admitted. 'It seemed probable that you would eventually reach this spot.' His regard this morning was fathomless. 'So, how do you find our home?'

'It's truly beautiful,' she acknowledged. 'A dream of a place! Why didn't you tell me you were a Count?' she tagged on.

He gave a brief shrug. 'I have no use for status symbols.'

'Ottavia doesn't appear to share the aversion.'

'My sister clings to an order long gone.' He patted the seat at his side. 'Come sit with me.'

'I have to get back,' she said hurriedly. 'It must be getting on for breakfast time.'

'Food will be served whenever and wherever required,' he advised. A hint of amusement in his eyes now, he added, 'You are afraid of me, perhaps?'

'Of course not!' she denied.

'Then, of what I make you feel?' he continued imperturbably.

Pretending not to know what he was talking about would be a waste of time and breath, Gina knew. 'You take a great deal too much for granted,' she retorted.

The amusement grew. 'That is your English half speaking. Your Barsini blood responds to mine.'

The time to tell him the truth was now, but the words wouldn't form themselves.

'Grateful as I am to you for what you're doing with my

car, I'm not about to become your playmate for the week,'
she said coolly instead.

'Playmates are for children,' he returned, not in the least
rebuffed. 'We are neither of us that.'

'But we *are* strangers,' she replied with deliberation.
'You don't really know anything about me.'

'Then, tell me,' he invited.

The moment was there again, but Gina still couldn't
bring herself to take advantage of it.

'I should be getting back,' she repeated.

'Then, I will come with you,' he said.

He got to his feet, lean and lithe as a panther in the
black trousers and shirt. Gina steeled herself as he moved
to where she stood, but he made no attempt to touch her,
falling into step at her side as she turned back the way she
had come. Catching the faint scent of aftershave, she was
supremely conscious of the fact that she had yet to shower,
yet to put a brush to her hair.

'Are you always up this early of a morning?' she asked.

'I rise when I awaken,' he said easily. 'No later than
six, sometimes as much as an hour before that.'

'Even when you don't get to bed until the early hours?'

'A matter of custom. If I tire in the day I may take siesta.
It depends on my commitments.'

'I imagine those are extensive.'

'Not too much so.'

Doing her best to keep the conversational ball rolling,
she said, 'You speak excellent English.'

'But somewhat structured compared with the way you
speak, yes?'

Gina cast a glance at the chiselled profile, responding to
the curve of his lips. 'My old English teacher would approve every word. It's usually tourists who introduce bad
habits.'

'Few tourists find Vernici,' he said. 'It is off the regular routes.'

'I know. I had some difficulty finding it myself.'

It was Lucius's turn to slant a glance, expression curious. 'Why were you looking for Vernici at all if your father came from Naples.'

Do it now! an inner voice urged her, even as she mentally cursed the slip-up. 'Latterly,' she heard herself saying regardless. 'But he was apparently born in Vernici, so I thought it worth taking a look there too.'

'I see.' From his tone, it was obvious that he was wondering why she hadn't mentioned that fact last night. 'The name is unfamiliar to me,' he went on after a moment, 'but the older townsfolk will surely recall the family. I will have enquiries made.'

She was getting deeper and deeper into the mire, thought Gina unhappily. What the devil was wrong with her that she kept on fabricating things?

They had reached the front of the house. Lucius preceded her up the steps to open a door for her to pass through, too close by far for comfort as he followed her in. Soles wet from their passage across the grass, her sandals had no purchase on the terrazzo. Lucius shot out an arm as she skidded, hauling her up against him, his hand warm at her waist.

'You must take more care,' he said, making no immediate attempt to let her go again.

'I will,' Gina assured him. 'I'm fine now, thanks.'

His laugh was low, the brief pressure of his lips at her nape where the curtain of hair had parted stirring her blood in a manner she deplored.

'I'd prefer you didn't do that,' she got out.

He laughed again, but this time released her. Gina made herself meet the dark eyes. 'I realise you probably won't be used to it, but I'm telling you again that I'm not…available.'

'Do you not think that you might be the one now taking too much for granted?' Lucius returned with mock gravity.

'Am I?' she challenged, and saw the glint return.

'No. I would be only half a man if I could look at you and not want you in the instant, *cara*.' He gave her no time to reply—if she could have come up with a reply at all. 'I will begin enquiries about the Barsini family this very morning. I would hope to have news of them before the day is over.'

A forlorn hope, Gina reflected ruefully. The longer this charade of hers continued, the harder it became to revoke.

'There's something I—' she began, breaking off as Guido heaved into view.

'Something you…?' Lucius prompted.

She shook her head, courage lost. 'Forget it.'

Leaving him standing there, she ran lightly up the stairs to head for her room. The situation was becoming increasingly difficult. If it weren't for her lack of transport, she would be tempted to abandon the whole idea and return home. She was vitally attracted to a man who might just be a close blood relation, a man who was making no effort to conceal *his* objective. Even if there should prove to be no connection, she wasn't into the kind of casual, ships that pass in the night, relationship that was all Lucius would have in mind.

Despite last night's refusal, breakfast was brought to her at eight o'clock. Gina ate it out on the balcony, enjoying both the view and the warmth. The sky was so blue, the quality of light a joy in itself. It was possible that her father had viewed the same scene—perhaps even from this very room. Could she really bear, Gina asked herself, not to know for certain?

She went downstairs again with no notion of how she was going to spend the day. Wandering out to the terrace, she found Ottavia stretched out on a lounger beneath an opened umbrella. She was wearing a gold-lamé bikini that barely covered her voluptuous curves, her eyes shielded by designer sunglasses. Her toenails, Gina noted, were painted the same shade of scarlet as her fingernails and lips, the whole effect more reminiscent of the film world, she thought, than Italian aristocracy.

'*Buon giorno,*' she proffered tentatively.

Ottavia pulled down the sunglasses a fraction to run a disparaging eye over the cotton dress Gina had elected to wear. 'You are quite recovered from your weariness, I trust?' she enquired, without bothering to respond to the greeting.

'Quite, thank you,' Gina confirmed. She felt it necessary to add, 'The breakfast was very good, but I really don't expect to be waited on while I'm here.'

'As you are here at my brother's invitation, you are entitled to be treated as any other guest,' came the smooth reply. 'You realise, of course, how fortunate you are to have gained his support in this affair.' She didn't wait for any answer. 'A word of warning, however. Lucius may pay you some attentions because he is a man and you are attractive to look at, but it means nothing.'

'In other words, don't run away with the idea that he might be about to offer marriage,' Gina returned. 'I'll certainly bear it in mind.'

The irony left no visible impression. 'Good,' was the only comment.

Her presence wasn't exactly welcome, Gina gathered, as the glasses were replaced and the head returned to the supporting cushion. She was tempted to stay anyway, just for the hell of it, but there was little to be gained from keeping company with someone who so obviously didn't want her there.

She had only covered a small part of the immediate grounds earlier. Now would be the right time to take a turn round the other side of the house before the heat became too great for comfort. With several days to fill, and nowhere else to go, she was probably going to be spending a lot of time out of doors. Which in this climate would be no great hardship, she had to admit.

She was crossing the drive when a low-slung sports car came roaring round the bend. Gina leapt instinctively for safety, missed her footing and went down on one knee in the gravel, steeling herself for the impact she was sure was to come. The car screeched to a halt with its front bumper bare inches from her. Spouting Italian at a rate of knots, the driver leapt out without bothering to turn off the engine, a look of concern on his handsome face as he came to lift her to her feet.

'*Inglese,*' Gina said for what seemed like the millionth time in response to what she took to be a spate of solicitous enquiry. '*Non capisco.*'

'English!' he exclaimed on a note of surprise.

'That's right.' Gina gave a wry grimace as she eased her knee. 'Does everybody round here drive like bats out of hell?'

His brows drew together in puzzlement. 'Bats?'

'It's just a saying,' she explained, regretting the use of it. 'It means fast, that's all.'

The frown cleared. 'Ah, fast!' Concern leapt once more in his eyes as he caught sight of the trickle of blood running down her leg. 'You are hurt! Why did you not tell me you were hurt?'

'I hadn't realised it was grazed,' Gina admitted, lifting the edge of her skirt to view the not inconsiderable damage. 'I thought I'd just knocked it.'

'It must be cleaned and dressed,' he declared. 'Before it becomes infected.'

'It will be,' she assured him. 'Just as soon as I get back to the house. I'm a guest there,' she added, in case he was in any doubt. 'Gina Redman.'

'A friend of the family?' He sounded intrigued.

'Not exactly. There was an accident. My car was badly damaged. Lu—Signor Carandente very generously invited me to stay until it's repaired.'

His lips curved. 'But of course. Lucius is the most generous of men. I am Cesare Traetta. You must allow me to drive you to the villa.'

'It's hardly any distance,' Gina protested. 'I might get blood on the upholstery.'

'If so it will be cleaned.' He went to open the passenger door. 'Please to get in.'

Gina wiped away the trickle of blood with her handkerchief before doing so. The soft leather seat cocooned her, its contours designed to hold the body in position. Definitely needed, she thought, as Cesare set the car into motion again with a force that caused the rear wheels to spin. She judged him around Lucius's age, which made him Donata's senior by fifteen years, yet the two of them appeared to be on a par when it came to road sense.

They rounded the final bend to come to a further screeching stop outside the house. Switching off the engine, Cesare got swiftly from the car to help Gina from the seat she was struggling to vacate without having her skirt ride up any further than it already had.

'I think I can manage, thanks,' she said drily when he

made to assist her up the steps. 'A damp flannel, and I'll
be as good as new!'

'You are bleeding!' exclaimed Lucius from the doorway, startling her because she hadn't seen him arrive.
'What happened to you?'

'I slipped and fell on the drive.' Gina saw no reason to
go into greater detail. 'Signor Traetta was kind enough to
give me a lift.'

'Cesare,' urged the man at her back. 'You must call me
Cesare.'

She gave him a brief smile. 'Cesare, then.' To Lucius
she said, 'I'll go and clean myself up.'

'The necessary materials will be brought to you.' he
said. 'We must be sure no foreign substances remain in
the wound.'

'Of course.' Gina was fast tiring of the fuss. 'I can
cope.'

'I am sure of it.' His tone was dry. 'Your self-sufficiency
does you credit. You will, however, wait for assistance in
this matter.'

He took her agreement for granted, indicating that she
precede him into the house. Gina battened down her instincts and meekly obeyed. 'I'm sure you know best,' she
murmured in passing, tongue tucked firmly in cheek.

The dress was not only dirty but torn at the hem, she
found on reaching her room. Not beyond repair, she supposed, examining the rip, though she was no expert needle-
woman. At any rate, she had plenty of other things to
change into, so it could wait until she got home.

Despite instructions, she ran hot water in the bathroom
basin and began cleaning off the worst of the mess. The
graze was quite extensive, with tiny pieces of gravel em-
bedded in the shredded flesh. Concentrating on extracting

them, she was taken unawares when Lucius entered the room bearing a first-aid box.

'You were to wait until I brought this!' he exclaimed.

Seated on a padded stool, her foot raised on the bath edge to enable her to see what she was doing, Gina resisted the urge to pull down the skirt she had raised to mid thigh.

'I hardly expected you to bring it up yourself,' she said lamely.

Dark brows rose. 'You think such a task beneath me?'

'Well, no, not exactly. I just took it…' She left the sentence unfinished, holding out her hand for the box. 'It's very good of you, anyway.'

Lucius made no attempt to hand it over. Placing it on the long marble surface into which the double basins were set, he seized soap from the dish and washed his hands. Gina watched in silence, reminded that she should have done the same before attempting to touch the graze at all.

His presence in the confines of the bathroom—spacious though it was—made her nervous. She found it difficult to control the quivering in her limbs when he took a pair of tweezers from the box and sat down on the bath edge to start work on the gravel.

The hand he slid about the back of her calf to hold her leg still was warm and firm against her skin, his fingers long and supple, the nails smoothly trimmed; she could imagine the way they would feel on her body—the sensual caresses. Her nipples were peaking at the very notion.

Stop it! she told herself harshly, ashamed of the sheer carnality of her thoughts. It might be a long-established fact that women were as capable as men of enjoying sex without love, but she had never followed the trend. From her mid teens she had determined not to settle for anything less than the real thing: the kind of love her mother had known for Giovanni Carandente. The possibility that

Lucius could be her father's nephew was enough on its own to prohibit any notion she might have of relaxing her ideals.

'I am sorry if I hurt you,' Lucius apologised as her leg jumped beneath his hands. 'There are only a few more small pieces to come, and then we are finished but for the antiseptic.'

'No problem,' she assured him. 'You're being very gentle. It's quite a mess, isn't it? I didn't realise how deep some of the bits had gone.'

'Thankfully, there should be no lasting scars,' he said without looking up from his task. 'It would be a pity to mar such a lovely leg.'

'Don't you ever stop?' she asked with a sharpness she hadn't intended.

This time he did look up, expression quizzical. 'You find my admiration irksome?'

Gina drew a steadying breath. 'I find it a little too…practised, that's all.'

'Ah, I see. You think I express the same sentiments to all women.' The dancing light was in his eyes again. 'Not so.'

He was hardly going to admit it, Gina told herself as he turned his attention once more to her knee. Not that it made any difference.

The antiseptic stung like crazy, but Lucius made no concessions. He finished the dressing with an expertly applied bandage.

'You may remove the dressing tomorrow to allow the healing tissue to form,' he said, relinquishing his hold on her at last.

Gina got to her feet to try a somewhat stiff-legged step, pulling a face at her reflection in the mirrored wall. 'I haven't had a bandaged knee since I was eight!'

'Long skirts, or the trousers women everywhere appear to have adopted, will cover your embarrassment.'

The dry tone drew her eyes to the olive-skinned face reflected in the mirror. 'You disapprove of the trend?' she asked lightly.

'I prefer a woman to dress as a woman,' he confirmed. 'As most men would say if asked.'

'Donata wears them,' Gina felt bound to point out, stung a little by the implied criticism. 'With that attitude, I'm surprised you allow it—to say nothing of the rest!'

'I said preference not outright rule,' came the steady response. 'Assuming that by the "rest" you refer to the state of my sister's hair, no amount of castigation can hasten the regrowth.'

Gina turned impulsively to face him, ashamed of the dig. 'I spoke out of turn. You said yesterday that she'd recently returned from school?'

The smile was brief and lacking in humour. 'She was despatched from her school for behaviour no reputable establishment could tolerate.'

'Not just for a haircut, surely!'

'A minor transgression compared with breaking out of the school in order to attend a nightclub in the nearby town. Not for the first time it appears. This time she was caught by the police when they raided the place in search of drugs.'

Gina gazed at him in dismay. 'You're not saying Donata was actually taking them?'

'She assures me not.'

'You do believe her?'

Lucius lifted his shoulders, mouth wry. 'I hardly know what to believe. I bitterly regret allowing her to persuade me into sending her to Switzerland at all. Her education was complete enough without this "finishing" she was so anxious to acquire.'

'She can't have been the only one to kick over the traces,' Gina ventured.

'If by that you mean was she alone on the night in question, the answer is no. There were two others caught with her. One American girl, one English. They too were despatched to their respective homes.'

'I see.' Silly as it seemed, Gina felt like apologising for the part the English girl had played. 'I don't suppose it helps much.'

'No,' Lucius agreed. 'I am still left with the problem of a sister turned insurgent. While she resides here at Cotone I can demand that she obeys certain rules of conduct, but there are limits to the penalties I can impose should she choose to defy me.'

'I can appreciate that,' Gina said carefully. 'It isn't as if she's a child any more.'

'She is eighteen years of age,' he advised on a harder note. 'By now she should be looking towards marriage and children of her own!'

'Marriage isn't the be all and end all of every woman's ambition.' Gina felt moved to protest, turning a deaf ear to the faint, dissenting voice at the back of her mind.

The dark eyes regarded her with a certain scepticism in their depths. 'You intend to stay single all your life?'

'I didn't say that. It depends whether I meet a man I want to marry.'

'And whom, of course, also wishes to marry you.'

'Well, obviously.' The mockery, mild though it was, stirred her to like response. 'Two hearts entwined for all eternity! Worth waiting for, wouldn't you say?'

'The heart has only a part to play,' he said. 'The body

and mind also have need of sustenance. The woman I myself marry must be capable of satisfying every part of me.'

'Typical male arrogance!' She exploded, driven beyond endurance by the sheer complacency of the statement. 'It would serve you right if...' She broke off, seeing the sparkle of laughter dawn and realising she'd been deliberately goaded. 'Serve you right if you were left high and dry!' she finished ruefully. 'Not that it's likely, I admit.'

The sparkle grew. 'You acknowledge me a man difficult for any woman to resist?'

'I acknowledge you a man with a lot more than just looks going for him, Count Carandente,' she said with delicate emphasis.

If she had been aiming to fetch him down a peg or two, she failed dismally. His shrug made light of the dig. 'Despite Ottavia's claim, the woman I marry will not carry the title of Contessa because she will be no more entitled to do so in reality than anyone in the last few hundred years. As I told you this morning, it is simply a status symbol. One for which I have little use myself.

'Which leaves me,' he went on with a wicked gleam, 'with just the looks you spoke of going for me. The looks that warm both your English and your Italian blood to a point where the differences no longer have bearing. Or would you still try to deny what lies between us, *cara*?'

The pithy response that trembled on her lips as he moved purposefully towards her was rejected as more likely to inflame than defuse the situation. What was she doing indulging in the kind of repartee scheduled to bring this very situation about to start with? she asked herself.

'Whatever you have in mind, you can forget it!' she said with what certainty she could muster, resisting any urge to try fighting him off physically as he drew her to him. 'I already told you, I'm not playing!'

'Words! Just words!' He put a forefinger beneath her chin to lift it, bending his head to touch his lips to hers with a delicacy that robbed her of any will to resist.

She was conscious of nothing but sensation as he kissed her: the pounding of her blood in her ears, the warmth spreading from the very centre of her body, the growing weakness in her lower limbs urging her to give way to the need rising so suddenly and fiercely in her. He drew her closer, moulding her to the contours of his masculine shape—making her aware of his own arousal in a manner that inflamed her even further. The words he murmured against her lips transcended all language barriers.

This man might be a close relative, came the desperate reminder, pulling her up as nothing else could have done right then.

'That's enough,' she got out, jerking away from him. 'In fact, it's more than enough!'

Anticipating at the very least a show of frustrated anger at her withdrawal from what must have appeared a near foregone conclusion, she was taken totally aback when Lucius simply laughed and shook his head.

'I think not, for either of us, but there is no haste. You will find Cesare and myself on the terrace should you care to join us for refreshment. He will be anxious to know that you suffered no long-lasting injury.'

He gathered the items he had taken from the first-aid box, and departed, leaving Gina standing there feeling all kinds of an idiot. Aroused he might have been, but he was obviously more than capable of controlling it. He certainly wouldn't demean himself by insisting on satisfaction, however encouraged to believe it forthcoming.

Telling him the truth now, and discovering that there was indeed a close blood relationship, could only prove embarrassing for them both. Probably the best thing she could do was forget the whole affair and head for home as soon as her car was repaired.

And spend the rest of her life wondering, came the thought. She was Giovanni Carandente's daughter. Having finally started on the quest, she had to see it through to the end, no matter what. There must be some way of finding out if this really was his place of origin that didn't involve giving herself away.

Her inclination was to spend the rest of the morning right here in her room, but that was no way for a guest to behave. With the bandage in mind, she donned a long, sarong-type skirt along with a silky vest, and slid her feet into a pair of thonged sandals. Not exactly haute couture, but it served the purpose.

Hair loose about her shoulders, face free of make-up apart from a dash of lipstick, she hid behind a pair of tortoiseshell sunglasses on going out to the terrace. Not just Lucius and Cesare to face, she saw, but Ottavia and Donata into the bargain, the former now fully and beautifully dressed.

Wearing a pair of deck trousers and a T-shirt, her hair raked through with a careless hand, Donata looked hardly less of the teenage rebel than she had in the leather outfit yesterday. She viewed Gina's arrival with a marked lack of enthusiasm.

Not so, Cesare, who leapt to see her seated with a solicitude that went down like a lead balloon with both sisters.

'Your leg must be supported,' he urged, raising the chair's built-in foot rest for her. 'You are in much pain?'

'None at all,' Gina assured him, submitting to his ministrations only because it was marginally less awkward than asking him to desist.

'I ordered fresh orange juice for you,' said Lucius as

one of the younger male staff members came from the house bearing a loaded tray. 'It can, of course, be replaced by something stronger if you prefer.'

'Thanks, but this is just what I need,' Gina assured him as the tall, ice-cool glass was set before her. She seized on it gratefully, sending a good quarter of the contents down her throat in one gulp.

'Iced drinks should be sipped so that the stomach suffers no sudden shock,' commented Donata with a certain malice. 'Isn't that so, Lucius?'

'Advisable, perhaps,' he agreed easily. 'If you are finding the heat overpowering we can move to a cooler part of the terrace,' he said to Gina herself.

The only heat she found overpowering was the kind he generated, came the fleeting thought. 'I find it no problem at all,' she assured him. 'I always did enjoy the sun.'

'What little you see of it in England.'

'Oh, we have our good days,' she returned lightly. 'Sometimes several together. You've visited my country?'

'Never for any length of time.'

'Tomorrow is the Palio,' Cesare put in with an air of being left too long on the sidelines. 'I have grandstand seats long-reserved should anyone care to share them.'

'*Si!*' declared Donata before anyone else could speak. '*Vorrei andare!*'

Lucius said something in the same language, wiping the sudden animation from her face. Pushing back her chair, she got jerkily to her feet and stalked off, mutiny in every line of her body.

'What exactly is the Palio?' asked Gina in the following pause, feeling a need for someone to say something.

It was Cesare who answered. 'A horse race run twice a year between Siena's *contrade*. Riders must circuit the

Piazza del Campo three times without the benefit of sad-
dles.'

'A bareback race!' Gina did her best to sound enthused.

'A little more than just that,' said Lucius. 'The city's
seventeen districts compete for a silk banner in honour of
the Virgin. A tradition begun many centuries ago. The race
itself lasts no more than a minute or two, but the pageantry
is day long. You might enjoy it.'

'You were only there the one time yourself that I recall,'
said Cesare. 'Why do we not all of us attend together?'

'It has become a tourist spectacle,' declared Ottavia dis-
dainfully. 'I have no desire to be part of it. Nor, I am sure,
will Marcello.'

'Then, perhaps the three of us,' he suggested, undeter-
red. 'Gina cannot be allowed to miss such an event.'

If Lucius refused too, it would be down to the two of
them next, Gina surmised, not at all sure she would want
to spend a whole day in Cesare's company. Equal though
he appeared to be in age to her host, he lacked the maturity
that was an intrinsic part of Lucius's appeal.

'The three of us, then,' Lucius agreed, to her relief. 'Providing that I drive us there. I would prefer that we arrive
without mishap.'

Cesare laughed, not in the least put out. 'You have so
little faith in me, *amico*, but I accept your offer.'

It had been an ultimatum not an offer, but Lucius obviously wasn't about to start splitting hairs. Gina found
herself wishing it was just going to be the two of *them*
taking the trip. Safer this way though, she acknowledged
ruefully. With Cesare around to act as chaperon, there
would be no repeat of this morning's assault on her senses.
Whichever way things might turn out, she was in no position to risk that kind of involvement.

CHAPTER THREE

CESARE took his departure shortly afterwards, accompanied by Lucius who wished to discuss some obviously private matter with him. Left alone with Ottavia, Gina made an effort to open a conversation, but soon gave up when her overtures failed to draw more than the briefest of replies.

'I think I'll go and find that cooler spot Lucius mentioned,' she said at length, getting to her feet. 'It's too hot to even think straight out here.'

The older woman made no reply at all to that; Gina hadn't really expected one. She could understand Donata's attitude regarding her presence in the house, but what axe did Ottavia have to grind?

There had been neither sight nor mention of Cornelia so far this morning. Either she was a late riser, or had gone out, Gina surmised. It still needed half an hour or so to noon. Lunch, she imagined, wouldn't be served much before one-thirty or even two. Not that she was hungry yet, but there was a lot of day still to get through.

The coolest place at this hour was going to be indoors. She went in via the glass doors to the *salotto*, welcoming the immediate flow of cooler air from the overhead fans. Reaching the hall, she stood for a moment wondering in which direction to head. Of the rooms that opened off it, she had so far only seen the one she had just come through and the library where she had first run into Lucius.

Feeling a bit of an intruder still, she opened a door under the right wing of the staircase, looking in on a small room

that appeared at first glance to be something of a deposi-
tory for unwanted items of furniture, with little in the way
of style about it.

About to close the door again, she paused as her eye
caught a reflection in the mirror almost directly opposite.
Eyes closed, Donata was seated in a high-backed chair that
concealed her from casual observation. From the look of
her, she had been crying.

It was likely that her company would be far from welcome, Gina reckoned, but she found herself stepping quietly into the room and easing the door to again regardless.
What she was going to say or do she had no clear idea.

The floor in here was laid in parquetry, the design
largely obscured by the heavy pieces of furniture. Donata
opened her eyes at the sound of footsteps, coming jerkily
to her feet as she registered the identity of the intruder.

'Leave me alone!' she urged. 'You have no right to be
here!'

Still not at all certain just what it was she hoped to
achieve, Gina halted a short distance away. 'I know I
haven't' she said, 'but, as I am, supposing we bury the
hatchet?'

Distracted by the unfamiliar phrase, Donata drew her
brows together. 'Bury the hatchet?'

'It means we forget about the accident and start again.
I'd rather be your friend than your enemy.'

A variety of expressions chased across the younger
girl's face as she gazed in silence for a moment or two.
When she did finally speak, the belligerence seemed almost forced. 'Why should *you* wish to be my friend?'

Why indeed? Gina asked herself, answering the question
in the same breath: because in all probability they shared
the same genes—or some of them, at any rate.

'I suppose I just don't like being disliked by anyone,'

she said on a semi-jocular note. 'Not that I'm having much success where your sister's concerned either.'

'Ottavia has little concern for anyone but herself,' declared Donata with unconcealed animosity. 'What *she* would most like is to be in Lucius's place.'

Gina could imagine. As *padrone*, Lucius would have total control of all Carandente affairs. Playing second fiddle wouldn't come easy to a woman of Ottavia's temperament. She wondered fleetingly what had prompted her to marry a man who appeared to be little more than an employee of the estate. It could hardly have been for lack of any other choice.

'You must miss your father,' she said softly, changing tack. 'How long is it since you lost him?'

The question took Donata by surprise; her response was automatic. '*Padre* died six years ago.'

'He can't have been all that old.'

'He was forty-eight.'

Which meant there had been just seven years between him and Giovanni Carandente, Gina calculated. Not that the knowledge brought her any closer to either proving or disproving a family connection.

'A big responsibility for your brother to take on so young,' she said. 'Especially as the last in line. It must put a lot of pressure on him.'

Donata eyed her suspiciously. 'Why should it matter to you?'

'It doesn't,' Gina hastened to assure her. 'I was just musing, that's all. It was very rude of me to make any comment at all on your family affairs.' She made a wry gesture. 'I'd better go. I shouldn't have intruded on you in the first place.'

'Then, why did you?'

'I could see you were upset.' Gina hedged. 'I couldn't just leave you like that.'

'You thought your offer of friendship all the comfort needed?'

Gina paid no heed to a sarcasm that had little real bite to it. 'Not all, but perhaps a little.' She hesitated before taking the plunge, aware of treading on delicate ground. 'Lucius told me what happened to you. It must have been a dreadful experience.'

The sympathy had an unexpected effect. Donata's face suddenly crumpled. 'He believes I took drugs!'

'I'm sure he doesn't.' Gina resisted the urge to go and put her arms about the girl. 'You just happened to be caught in the wrong place at the wrong time. It's only been a few days. He'll get over being angry about it.'

'No, he won't.' The tears were threatening to spill again, all trace of insurgency vanished. 'He can't bear even to look at me! No one can!'

And therein, thought Gina in swift understanding, lay the true source of misery. She kept her tone calm and level. 'Because of your hair, you mean?'

'Yes. It was like yours before I allowed Meryl to take scissors to it. She told me it would look so much smarter cut short.'

'Meryl is a hairdresser?'

'No, she was my friend.'

Some friend! Gina reflected. 'A very jealous one, I'd say,' she observed. 'It's going to take time to grow back,' she went on, seeing no point in pretending otherwise, 'but it could be made to look much better than it does.'

Faint hope dawned in the girl's eyes. 'You could do this?'

It wasn't exactly what Gina had had in mind, but she could scarcely make a worse job of it, she decided. 'I can try,' she said. 'You should really have a properly qualified stylist take a look at it.'

'Now is the most important,' declared Donata with growing eagerness. 'If I look less like the scarecrow Lucius called me, he might allow me to accompany you to the Palio tomorrow. He likes you very much, I can tell. He would listen if you asked him.'

Gina very much doubted it, but she couldn't find it in herself to refuse the request out of hand. 'I can but try,' she said again.

'Thank you.' The smile was radiant. 'And I'm truly sorry about your car. It *was* all my fault. I was driving recklessly.'

'Don't worry about it.' Gina could hardly credit the change in the girl. 'I'm sure it will come back as good as new. Anyway, we'd better get to it if we're to be through before lunch.'

'Luncheon is at two o'clock,' Donata confirmed. 'Almost two hours away yet.'

Almost two hours to effect a make-over that would persuade Lucius to relent; Gina only hoped she was up to it.

It took every minute, and some judicious snipping, to achieve anything of a success. By the time she'd finished blow-drying the thick dark mass, she was beginning to regret ever having got involved.

She drew a breath of cautious relief on viewing the finished product. With the layers given some shape and lift, and shorter fronds framing the face, it was no salon creation, but it was certainly a vast improvement. Donata seemed pleased enough with it, at any rate.

At Gina's suggestion, she exchanged the deck trousers for a cream linen skirt, the T-shirt for a pale green blouse. She was, she declared extravagantly, happy to accept any advice from someone she now regarded as the only true friend she had ever known.

Something of an achievement in less than twenty-four hours, Gina supposed. She hoped Lucius wouldn't see it as presumption on her part.

Lunch was served on a side terrace beneath a projecting canopy. Ottavia viewed her sister's transformation with limited interest. Better than no effort at all, she said, though hardly a cause for celebration.

It was left to Lucius to express a more complimentary opinion. All the same, Gina had the feeling that he didn't really like the idea of her pitching in on a family affair. In which case, he should have kept his mouth shut about the whole thing, she told herself stoutly.

With Donata urging her in every way without actually saying anything, Gina collared him straight after the meal before she could lose courage.

'About tomorrow,' she began.

'You no longer wish to see the Palio?' Lucius asked.

'Yes, of course I do.' She paused, sidetracking for the moment. 'Although I'd hate to feel I was dragging you away from more important matters. I'm grateful for what you're already doing. I certainly don't expect you to provide entertainment too.'

'I have no other commitment,' he assured her. 'Unless you would prefer to spend the day with Cesare alone?'

'Oh, no!'

The denial was quick—too quick—drawing a smile to his lips. 'Then, where is the problem?'

'Donata hopes to come with us.'

'Commendable though your efforts to improve her appearance are,' he said on a suddenly curious note, 'I find myself asking why you would go to such lengths for someone who has given you nothing but aggravation?'

'I can't help feeling some sympathy for her,' Gina admitted truthfully. 'She's young for her age, and impressionable. I'd say this friend of hers—Meryl—has a lot to answer for. She was the one who persuaded her to have a hair cut. She was probably the one who instigated the break-out in the first place. Some people get a lot of pleasure out of leading others astray.'

'You appear to speak with some authority,' he said.

'I went through a bad phase myself in my teen years through mixing with the wrong kind of people—' she forbore from mentioning that she had been just fourteen at the time '—so I do have some insight into what's been driving Donata since she came home.' Gina had the bit too firmly between her teeth to consider letting go now. 'She's simply living up to the image she believes everyone has of her. What she needs is a little compassion. Did you never get yourself into unfortunate situations when you were a boy?'

'Nothing of any great note.' There was no telling what Lucius was thinking or feeling. 'You consider me lacking in humanity, then?'

Gina eyed him uncertainly, aware of having rather overstepped the mark as a mere guest in the house. 'I think you're probably finding it a difficult situation to deal with all round,' she said at length, feeling it a bit late to start apologising. 'Your mother, or Ottavia, would surely be better equipped.'

'Not all women are necessarily attuned to others,' came the dry return. 'You are certainly the most outspoken I have met.'

'I never did know when to mind my own business,' she

admitted, going for a lighter note. 'Forget I spoke, will you?'

The strong mouth slanted. 'I would find that difficult indeed. You may tell Donata you succeeded in convincing me of my harshness in refusing her request to attend the Palio.'

'Thank you.' Gina was taken aback by the sudden capitulation. 'I'm sure she'll really appreciate it.'

'I doubt that Cesare will share the feeling.'

'Oh?' She searched the olive features. 'Why not?'

Lucius lifted expressive shoulders. 'Donata has had what I believe is termed a crush on him since she was sixteen. She counted, I think, on this year in Switzerland turning her into the kind of woman he would want for a wife.'

'Cesare knows how she feels?'

'Of course. He used to find it amusing, but not so much now.'

'You should have said.'

'And have you accuse me of putting Cesare's feelings before those of my own sister?' he responded with irony. 'No, he must find it in himself to bear with the situation. Unless, of course, you can make use of this rapport the two of you appear to have formed to persuade her of her foolishness in pursuing a man so many years her senior.'

'I really did jump in with both feet, didn't I?' Gina said wryly. 'I don't imagine anything I could say would change the way she feels.'

'It can do no harm to try.'

Gina regarded him in some doubt. 'You seriously want me to talk to her?'

'It can do no harm,' Lucius repeated. 'She has somehow to be convinced that Cesare will never see her in the way she wants him to see her.'

'She'd have to accept it if he married someone else,' she said. 'Is that likely to be happening in the near future?'

'Not that I am aware of.'

'I suppose, like you, he's looking for an ideal.' Gina kept her tone light. 'I saw a film not so long ago where women were turned into robots programmed to satisfy a man's every desire.'

Amusement sparkled in the dark eyes. 'An on-off switch might have its uses at times, but my needs would be far from satisfied by programmed compliance.'

They were still seated at table. Gina resisted the urge to snatch her hands away as he reached across to take them in his.

'So smooth and lovely!' he murmured.

'I thought we were discussing your sister,' she said, willing herself to reveal no hint of the turbulence his very touch aroused in her. 'I'm no agony aunt, but I'll give it a go.'

Lucius raised a brow. 'Agony aunt?'

'They give advice to people who write in with problems. I imagine magazines over here have them too.' Gina could no longer contain her quivering reaction to the gentle circling of his fingertip in the centre of her palm. 'Don't!' she said huskily.

Lucius complied at once, sitting back in his seat to regard her with a quizzical expression. 'What is it that you fear about me, *cara*? That I may pass on some dread disease?'

'It hadn't even occurred to me.' She could say that in all honesty. She made herself look him in the eye. 'I just don't like being taken for granted, that's all.'

'I take nothing for granted, if by that you mean you believe me convinced of my ability to conquer,' he responded equably. 'I make no secret of the fact that I find you desirable because I see no point in pretending otherwise, but there is little pleasure to be gained from a foregone conclusion. Would you deny your own desires?' he continued when she made no reply. 'Are you telling me that your response to my touch is a figment of my imagination?'

Gina lifted her shoulders, fighting to stay on top of her warring emotions. 'I find you physically attractive, yes. That doesn't necessarily mean I want to jump into the nearest bed with you.'

'It doesn't mean that you *have* to jump into bed with me,' Lucius amended. 'Could it be that you fear being thought a woman of easy virtue if you give way to your urges?'

'Isn't that the way a lot of men still secretly feel about women who do?' she challenged.

'I can speak only for myself. I find nothing wrong with a woman indulging her needs.'

'Even the one you eventually marry?'

'Ah!' The exclamation was soft. 'That would be a different matter.'

'That's sheer hypocrisy!' Gina accused.

'Perhaps,' he returned. 'I make no claim to faultlessness. The mother of my children will have known no other man but me.'

He meant it, she realised. Every word! 'If you're planning on a family, you're leaving it rather late to get started, aren't you?' she said with a tartness that fired a sudden spark in his eyes.

'I doubt that my ability to father a child is much impaired. As to the woman I do take to wife, she will obviously be young enough to bear as many babies as it takes to produce a son who will carry on the name of Carandente.'

'It's all so damned clinical!' Gina could scarcely contain her repugnance. 'I pity whoever you do marry. I really do!'

This time he showed no visible reaction. 'There are many who will envy her the life she will lead. Many who would all too willingly take her place.'

'Fine.' Gina pushed back her chair to get to her feet, the scorn in her voice reflected in her eyes. 'Gives you plenty of choice, then. I'm going to take siesta, if that's all right?'

'But of course,' Lucius said smoothly, having risen to his feet with her. 'Perhaps we may talk again later when you are rested. There are matters we should have clear between us.'

Gina gave a brief nod, unable to trust her voice. She had gone beyond the boundaries again, and this time a little too far for comfort. Lucius might not show it, but she could sense the anger in him at her unequivocal condemnation. Distasteful as she found his attitude, it was hardly her place to revile him for it. He would no doubt be pointing that out to her.

She made it to her room without running into Donata. Kicking off her sandals, she lay down on the bed, welcoming the airflow from above. This was only her second day at the villa, and already she had managed to alienate her host. She couldn't possibly stay on here now. She must find accommodation in town until repairs to her car were completed. No Palio trip for certain.

She hadn't expected to sleep, but she did, waking to the sound of a tentative knock on the door an hour or so later.

'Am I disturbing you?' asked Donata, hovering on the threshold.

The obvious answer was yes, but Gina hadn't the heart to say it. 'I was about to get up anyway,' she said instead, suiting her actions to her words. She pulled a wry face. 'I'm getting into bad habits sleeping in the middle of the day!'

'*Madre* always takes siesta,' rejoined the younger girl. 'She considers it essential for her well-being.'

'A matter of what you're used to, I suppose. Is your mother not at home today?' Gina added casually.

'She went to visit with friends in Umbria. She won't be at home for three more days.' The pause was brief, the anxiety spilling over. 'You asked Lucius about my accompanying you to the Palio?'

Gina hesitated, wondering how best to say what she had to say. 'I did,' she responded. 'But—'

'He said no!' Donata's face set into lines recognisable from the day before, her eyes glittering with resentment. 'I hate him!'

'As a matter of fact, he said yes. You didn't give me chance to finish. It will be just the three of you. I shan't be coming.'

Her fury dying as swiftly as it had arisen, Donata looked flatteringly disappointed. 'But why?'

'Because I've decided to move to Vernici first thing in the morning.'

Disappointment gave way to perplexity. 'But your car won't be ready for several more days at least.'

'I know. I just feel it too much of an imposition to stay here all that time. The car can be delivered straight to the garage in Vernici.'

'Lucius won't allow you to go,' Donata declared with confidence. 'He'll insist that you stay.'

Lucius, Gina reflected drily, would probably be happy to see the back of her. She'd blotted her copybook with a vengeance.

*   *   *

Dinner was an uncomfortable meal. Lucius treated her with no less courtesy than before, though there was precious little humour in the gaze he rested on her from time to time.

Donata waited until halfway through the meal before announcing Gina's intention of leaving the villa in the morning.

'She feels she is imposing,' she said. 'But she must stay, must she not, Lucius?'

'There can be no question of it,' he returned levelly. 'Vernici has no suitable hotel.'

'My standards aren't that high,' Gina interposed.

'Mine,' he declared, 'are very high. You will please not insult me by refusing to accept my hospitality.'

Gina met his eyes, flushing a little. 'I didn't mean to insult you.'

'Then, the matter is settled.'

Ottavia kept her own counsel, although Gina suspected that she for one would have been more than ready to see her depart. Short of simply walking out on the household, she really had little choice. Lucius might not be feeling too friendly towards her after her diatribe earlier, but his breeding prevailed. Like it or not, she was here for the duration.

Anticipating some eventual move on his part to take her aside for the clarification he had spoken of, she was on tenterhooks for the rest of evening. By the time they retired for the night she had come to the conclusion that he'd decided to let silence speak for itself. One thing did appear clear: there would be no further flirtation on his part. A relief, she told herself.

Morning brought a fresh dilemma. With no way of knowing whether the Palio trip was still on, she was uncertain of how to dress. Her now unbandaged but scabby knee ruled out any short skirts for certain. She settled in the end on the bottom half of a white linen-mix trouser suit, to which she could easily add the jacket if necessary, along with a sleeveless blue top for coolness.

She was just about ready to venture downstairs when Crispina arrived with breakfast. The note she brought with her was short and to the point. Cesare would be here at nine. There was no indication as to whether Lucius would be accompanying the party, but Gina believed it unlikely. Having breakfast sent to her room was probably his way of expressing his lack of desire to see her at all. She considered developing a sudden headache and crying off herself, but that was too much like crawling into a hole.

Convinced by the time she did go down at five minutes to the hour that Lucius would not be around, she was torn between conflicting emotions on finding him waiting with Donata and Cesare in the hall. Like the latter, he was wearing a lightweight suit in a neutral colour, both jacket and shirt collar left open. Two equally devastating males, Gina acknowledged, yet it was only the one who could make her heart beat faster.

Cesare greeted her with an admiration that was more than a little overdone in her estimation.

'*Bella!*' he exclaimed. '*Sfarzosa!* Your injury?' he added solicitously in English. 'It gives you no pain this morning?'

'None at all,' she assured him. 'It looked a lot worse than it actually was.'

'I thank the heavens that I caused you no greater hurt!'

Gina looked away from him to give Donata a smile, unsurprised to receive a somewhat strained response. Having the man of one's dreams show interest of any kind in another woman was bad enough; having him lay it on as thickly as he'd just done was too much altogether. Donata was, Gina suspected, already beginning to regret last night's eagerness to have her remain.

'Shall we go?' said Lucius crisply.

The car awaiting them out front was an opulent saloon that looked as if it had just been fetched from the show-room.

'Gina must sit up front with Lucius,' declared Donata, and made sure of it by sliding into a rear seat herself.

Looking resigned, Cesare saw Gina into the car while Lucius went round to get behind the wheel, then took his seat at Donata's side.

Gina did her best to relax as Lucius put the vehicle into motion, but it was impossible while the atmosphere between them remained so cool. If she was going to be here for several more days, then steps had to be taken to restore at least a measure of harmony. And it was up to her to make the move.

CHAPTER FOUR

DOMINATED by the sparkling white fantasy of its cathedral, Siena was a maze of narrow streets lined with Gothic mansions. Reaching the Campo to see the throng crushed into the centre where viewing was free of charge, Gina could only be thankful for the shade and relative comfort of their grandstand seats.

She took advantage of the first opportunity that arose to speak with Lucius out of earshot of the other two.

'I owe you an apology for what I said to you yesterday,' she tendered frankly. 'I was out of order.'

Expression enigmatic, he inclined his head. 'You are entitled to an opinion.'

'But not to express it in such a manner.' She made a rueful gesture. 'I really am sorry.'

A reassuring glimmer of humour lit the dark eyes. 'The humility is appreciated. So we are friends again, yes?'

Gina smiled back a little tentatively, wondering how he would react to the news that they possibly shared the same blood-line. 'Friends,' she agreed.

As promised, the day was full of spectacular pageantry, with costumed processions, flag-hurling and drumming. Gina enjoyed that far more than the race itself. A hectic, three-lap circuit with few holds barred, it left several horses and riders with injuries.

There would be another race in August, Lucius advised, with practice races and qualifying heats held between. By then this whole episode would be just a memory, Gina reflected dispiritedly.

Retracing their steps to the place where they had left the car proved no easy task in the milling throngs. Having paused for a moment to watch a puppet show in the belief that the others were at her back, she was surprised and a little perturbed to find herself apparently abandoned when she turned. She pushed on through the crowd in the direction she thought they had been taking, expecting to come on the three of them waiting for her to catch up at any moment.

It was a relief to see Cesare's face through the sea of heads, although he appeared to be approaching from a different direction altogether.

'I came back to find you,' he said on reaching her side. 'Lucius and Donata are waiting up ahead. To where did you vanish?'

'I stopped to look at a sideshow,' Gina admitted. 'I thought you'd all done the same. I was just about to start panicking,' she added with a laugh.

'There is no need now that I am with you,' Cesare assured her. He took her arm. 'We must go this way.'

Totally disorientated, Gina stuck to his side as he forged a passage through the crowds. Hard as she looked, she could catch no glimpse of either of the Carandentes.

'We must be going in the wrong direction!' she exclaimed after several fruitless minutes had elapsed. 'We'll never find them now!'

'We will all of us meet back at the car in due course,' Cesare consoled. 'At the moment you look very much in need of refreshment. A cool drink would be welcome, yes?'

Gina hesitated, torn between the urge to keep on searching, and the thirst she couldn't deny. It was so hot here in the midst of the surging throng, the humidity oppressive. Thirst won the battle. As Cesare had said, they would all meet at the car in due course. Meanwhile, a few minutes respite over a drink was surely going to make little difference.

They were lucky enough to slide into seats just vacated on the terrace of a nearby bar. Gina asked for a lager as the drink most likely to settle the dust in her throat, closing her eyes in near ecstasy as the icy cold liquid slid down.

'That,' she declared, setting her empty glass on the table, 'was pure nectar!'

'You would like another?' asked Cesare.

She shook her head. 'One's quite enough thanks. I'd hate to turn up at the car tipsy.' She eyed his own glass, which was still half full. 'How long do you think it will take us to get to where we left it?'

'It will depend,' he said, 'on whether I can accurately recall the exact street. Did you take note of the name yourself, by any chance?'

Gina shook her head again, this time in some alarm. 'It never occurred to me.'

'Nor to me. My mind was on other matters.' He made a wry gesture. 'I find it difficult to know how to deal with Donata's feelings for me. She is little more than a child!'

Gina hesitated before responding to the unspoken plea. 'In your estimation, perhaps, because you've probably known her all her life, but not in hers.'

'But I am almost twice her age!'

'Some girls go for older men. Especially those who've lacked a father figure, I've read.'

Cesare looked anything but flattered. 'Lucius has been a father to her these past six years since Paulo died.'

'Lucius is her brother. It's a totally different thing.'

'I have given her no cause to think of *me* in such a role!'

'It's only a suggestion,' Gina assured him. 'You don't exactly fit the image, I have to admit.'

A smile lit the handsome features. 'I would hope not indeed!' He viewed her with frank appreciation, gaze travelling from her face down the firm line of her throat to linger for a second or two on the thrust of her breasts. 'Lucius tells me you are half Italian yourself, with a father *you* never knew at all. Shall you continue to search for his family when your car is ready to drive again?'

'It depends how much time I have left,' she said. 'I'm due to start a new job in a couple of weeks.'

'You should stay here in Italy,' he returned caressingly. 'You belong in the sunlight, *cara*.'

Odd, thought Gina, how the same endearment could have such little impact when used by another man. Not that Lucius employed the word in any really meaningful sense either. It was just a term of address that came all too easily to male lips in this part of the world.

'I belong where I'm accustomed to being,' she said on a light note. 'I can't even speak the language.'

'The language of love is universal. We could speak it together, you and I.'

'We could, but we won't.' Gina was taking him no more seriously than his sparkling eyes indicated. 'Are you going to finish your drink?'

He gave a mock sigh. 'You will never know what you miss!'

'What I don't know can't be missed.' She let a moment or two pass while he took another pull at his glass before saying casually, 'How long *have* you known the Carandentes?'

'Since they first came to Tuscany seventeen years ago,' he acknowledged.

Gina felt her heart give a sudden lurch. 'So who owned San Cotone before they arrived?'

'Cotone has been in the family for many generations. As a distant cousin, Paulo was not in the direct line of inheritance, but he was the only one left to carry on the name.'

'What happened to the rest of them?'

'The son who should have been the next in line was killed some years before his father passed on. There was no other issue.' Cesare gave her a quizzical look. 'Lucius is the person to ask about the family history if it interests you.'

Grappling with the implications of what she'd just been told, Gina raised a smile and a shrug. 'Just plain old curiosity. I think it's time we went in search of the car, don't you?'

With the crowds still thick, and lacking a definite location, it took them more than half an hour to find the vehicle, and only then because Gina happened to recognise an ornate building on the corner of the street where they had parked. Donata was already seated inside the car, which was within shade; Lucius greeted the pair of them in mingled relief and annoyance.

'We,' he declared, 'have been waiting here for almost an hour! I was on the verge of calling for assistance in finding the two of you!'

'My fault,' claimed Cesare. 'I forgot to take note of the location. But for Gina's better senses, we could have wandered the streets for ever!'

'Sheer luck,' Gina disclaimed. 'It was my fault we got separated in the first place. I'd have been in real trouble without Cesare. I wouldn't even know how to say "I'm lost" in Italian!'

'A few basic phrases should be simple enough for even

the English to learn,' came the unsympathetic retort. Lucius opened the rear door, indicating that she should get into the car. 'We had best be on our way before the roads from the city become blocked with traffic, as will begin to happen very shortly.'

As was starting to happen already, if the route she and Cesare had just traversed was any example, Gina reflected. She weathered a glowering look from Donata as she slid into the seat at her side. The younger girl had nothing at all to worry about so far as she was concerned, but this was hardly the time or the place to tell her so. It was up to Cesare to put her straight with regard to his feelings— or lack of them. And the sooner the better.

There had been little opportunity up to now to go over the information Cesare had supplied. With Donata in no mood for conversation, she was able to put her mind to it at last. The coincidences were too many for there to be any mistake. The son who had been killed must have been her father. If Paulo Carandente hadn't been in the direct line of inheritance, then the blood connection between her and Lucius was too remote to be of any account.

So what now? she asked herself, thrusting that latter thought aside. If she told the truth she would not only be faced with the problem of explaining the fabrications, which would be difficult enough, but all the questions, the probing—the possible assumption that she was after financial gain. All she'd ever really wanted was to know where her father had come from. Why cause unnecessary disruption?

Cesare took off in his own car almost immediately on reaching the villa, leaving Donata to make what she would of his excuses for not staying longer. Now wasn't the time to try talking to her either, Gina reckoned, as the girl headed indoors without so much as a glance in her direction. Whatever rapport they had developed yesterday was right out of the window at present.

'I think she believes I'm interested in Cesare myself,' she remarked to Lucius as they followed her inside.

'And are you?' he asked.

Gina glanced his way uncertainly. 'Is that meant to be a joke?'

His mouth slanted. 'Why should I joke about such matters? Cesare has many admirers.'

'I don't doubt it,' she said. 'But I'm not one of them. Not in the way you mean, at any rate.'

Suit jacket slung casually over a shoulder, Lucius paused in the hall to view her with a certain cynicism. 'How many ways are there?'

'More than one, for certain,' she returned, not altogether sure where this was going. 'I like Cesare as a person, and he is very good-looking, but he doesn't attract me as a man.'

'But *I* do?'

Gina kept a tight rein on her impulses, lifting her shoulders in a brief shrug. 'In some respects.'

This time his smile was genuine. 'I would be interested to hear what you find disfavourable in me. Apart from the matters we discussed yesterday, that is.'

'Your arrogance, for one thing,' she said with purpose.

'You prefer a man who is unsure of himself?'

'Of himself, no. Of me, yes.'

'You believe me incapable of knowing what you are thinking, what you are feeling?' His voice had softened, his eyes acquiring an expression that set every nerve aquiver. He brought up a hand to trace the tip of a finger down the side of her face and across her lips. 'You feel the same desire I feel for you, *mi tesoro*. The desire we must both of us satisfy before too long.'

'I'm going to get a shower,' she said with what composure she could rally. 'I'd suggest you take a very cold one.'

His laughter followed her as she turned away to mount the stairs. Gina fought to stop herself from looking down on reaching the gallery, though her senses told her he was still standing there. Staying celibate was easy enough when there was no real temptation to do otherwise, but the whole idea of saving herself for Mr Right held little sway right now, she had to admit.

If the day had been long, the evening seemed to stretch to infinity. Donata was subdued, picking at her food with little interest. Nothing anyone could say was going to help, Gina judged. The girl had to come to terms with the unlikelihood of Cesare returning her feelings.

Used to eating no later than seven-thirty at home, unless being taken out to dinner, she found it difficult to accustom herself to a mealtime that not only started when she would normally be long finished, but could last into the small hours if the diners were of a mind. As always, wine flowed freely, with the house Chianti readily available.

'Would it be possible for me to see the vineyards?' she asked over coffee. 'I've never visited one before.'

'By all means,' Lucius said easily. 'I will show you them myself tomorrow.'

Gina met his eyes, unable to penetrate the dark depths. 'Thank you.'

'You will find it all very boring,' Ottavia advised. 'To see one grape is to see them all!'

'Gina will make her own assessment,' her brother responded. 'Perhaps you might like to take a walk around the gardens before we retire for the night?' he added on the same easy note.

Was there just the slightest emphasis on the 'we', Gina wondered, or was she reading too much into too little? She knew a sudden reckless surge. There was only one way to find out.

'I would, yes,' she said.

Lucius got to his feet, the coffee left in his cup ignored. 'Then, we will go now, while the mood is on us.'

Gina rose from the table to join him, keeping her expression under strict control as she sensed Ottavia's gaze. *'Buona sera,'* she murmured.

'Sera is evening, *notte* is night,' came the tart reply. 'Enjoy your stroll. The night air will, I am sure, aid restful sleep.'

Gina refused to let the suspected innuendo affect her. So what if Ottavia did have a notion of what was in her mind? Why should she care *what* the woman thought of her? Once she left here she would never see her again.

Lucius neither, came the thought, bringing a momentary despondency before her spirit reasserted itself. Forget next week. Concentrate on now.

The night was warm, the skies cloudless, the stars so much bigger and brighter than they ever appeared back home. Lucius made no immediate attempt to touch her in any fashion, strolling at her side much as he had done the previous morning, hands thrust into trouser pockets.

'There is a difference about you tonight,' he remarked shrewdly after a moment or two. 'Would I be wrong in thinking you ready to acknowledge what lies between us?'

'I decided it was time to start being honest with myself, yes,' she said, fighting the urge to run for safety while she still had the chance.

'You admit that you want me in the same way that I want you.' It was a statement not a question. 'What was it that made this decision for you?'

Gina gave a light shrug. 'I just saw no point in further pretence. After all, we're both adults.'

'True.' There was just the faintest trace of irony in his tone. 'So we waste no more time.'

Blood hammering in her ears as he drew her to him, nerves jumping all over the place, Gina met his lips, every last doubt vanishing at the first spine-tingling contact. The arms he slid about her were already possessive, drawing her close, making her feel his strength, his heat. She clung to him, lips opening to the silky pressure of his tongue, tasting him the way he was tasting her. There was no room for anything else in her mind but what was happening this very minute. She wanted what he wanted. *Everything* he wanted.

'Not here,' he murmured roughly. 'Come.'

They made it to her room without running into anyone, although by that time Gina was past caring.

Aroused though he was, Lucius refused to hurry, kissing her into a state where she hardly knew whether she was standing on her head or her heels before removing a single garment.

Nude, he was magnificent: a bronze statue come to full and vibrant life. Her skin looked almost translucent in contrast. She trembled to the feel of his hands as he slowly traced a passage down over her slender curves, breath catching in her throat when he slid a gentle finger between her thighs to penetrate her most intimate depths. She moved instinctively in rhythm with the motion, the tumult gathering until she could no longer contain it, overcome by wave after wave of overwhelming sensation.

Only then did he lower her onto the bed, supporting

himself on his forearms as he nuzzled her breasts. Gina opened her thighs to accommodate the burgeoning pressure, thrilling to the sheer weight of him, the size of him— moving her body in urgent seeking of even closer encounter.

It took her a moment to realise what was happening when he lifted himself away for a brief period. She hadn't even thought about protection until now, she realised. She forgot about it again almost instantly as he lowered himself back to her. The feeling as he slid inside her was indescribable. Flesh to flesh, spirit to spirit, came the hazy thought before everything merged into one great spinning Catherine wheel.

He was still there when she awoke at first light. For a moment or two she just lay studying his face, committing every wonderful, masculine line to memory. He had taken her to a place no amount of imagination could have painted for her, with little of the half anticipated pain to mar the moment of merging. Not that it wouldn't have been worth any amount of pain.

No regrets, she told herself firmly. And no backsliding on the decision previously made either. There was nothing to be gained from the truth.

She became suddenly aware that Lucius was awake, his eyes fired by the same memories as he looked back at her. His smile was a caress in itself.

'You,' he said softly, 'are a beautiful, warm and passionate woman, *cara mia*!'

'It must be the Italian in me,' she murmured, and saw the embers flare into vibrant life again.

The first time had been wonderful enough, but this surpassed it. If there had been any restraint left in her at all, she shed it in those tumultuous minutes, wrapping slender limbs about him as he came into her once more; loving his power, his passion, his very dominance.

They lay together in drowned repletion for some time afterwards. Gina was the first to stir, albeit with reluctance.

'I have to visit the bathroom,' she whispered.

Lucius kissed the tip of her nose before releasing her. 'I must leave you,' he said with obvious reluctance. 'The sun is already well-risen.'

He sat up as she slid from the bed, watching in some amusement as she pulled on a cotton wrap. 'A little late, I think, for such modesty. You have no secrets from me now.'

She had one, she thought wryly. 'Call it a foible,' she said. 'I'm not used to flaunting myself.'

'There is no shame in showing so beautiful a body. But the choice, of course, is your own.' He threw back the covers and rose to his feet, totally at ease with his own nudity. 'We will go to the winery immediately after breakfast,' he said, reaching for the clothing he had discarded in such haste a few hours ago.

Gina tore her eyes away from him with an effort, and headed for the bathroom. So far as Lucius knew, she had done nothing with him that she hadn't done with other men before him. All this talk about a man being able to tell when it was the first time for a woman was obviously rubbish. True, he'd made sure she was thoroughly aroused—which perhaps many men neglected to do.

The euphoria of a few minutes ago had diminished. While she couldn't bring herself to regret giving herself to him, he had probably set a precedent it was going to be difficult to match. It was also possible that having achieved his aim with so little effort, he would have no interest in pursuing it any further himself.

Expecting him to be gone when she returned to the bedroom to look out something to wear, she was surprised to find him standing fully dressed by the bed. The expression on his face unnerved her.

'Why did you make yourself out to be what you are not?' he asked softly.

For a fleeting moment she thought he was talking about the lie she had told, but he would hardly have waited until now to face her with it if he'd somehow learned the truth. Which left only one thing he could possibly mean.

There was no point in prevarication, but she found herself doing it anyway. 'What are you talking about?'

He stretched a finger to indicate a point on the bed. 'That.'

Gina moved forward reluctantly to view the exposed sheet, biting her lip on seeing the smear of blood. It hadn't occurred to her to even consider the possibility of such evidence appearing. Further denial was obviously useless. Lucius was fully aware of what the stain signified.

'Does it really matter?' she got out. 'I had to lose it sometime.'

'But why now, and to me?'

Gina tried a smile, a hint of irony. 'I hardly need to tell you what you're already well aware of.'

'You found me impossible to resist.'

'That's right.'

Lucius studied her hardily. 'If you waited this long, it can only be because you intended saving yourself for the man you marry.'

'I waited this long,' she said, 'because I never met anyone else who made me want it enough.'

'Or who could perhaps offer you sufficient return?'

Gina pushed a distracted hand through her hair, leaving it standing out in a dark cloud from her head. 'You can't possibly think—'

'I think it possible that our conversation the other after-noon may have led you to believe I would consider an offer of marriage obligatory in the circumstances.'

'That's ridiculous!' She could still scarcely credit the suggestion. 'I'm not looking for marriage with anyone!'

'You would refuse me, then?'

'You can count on it!' She was too furious to care what she said, or how she said it. 'You may consider yourself the catch of the century, but I'd be looking for a great deal more in a husband than *anything* you could offer! If you—'

'I take your word,' he interrupted drily. 'Although I would dispute the *anything*.'

Gina caught herself up, eyeing him in sudden confusion. 'If this is your idea of a joke, it certainly isn't mine!'

'No joke,' he assured her. 'Just a means of discovering the truth.' He paused, his expression difficult to read. 'If you had no thought of entering into a relationship before we met, I assume that you use no form of protection?'

'Does it matter?' she said again. 'You did.'

'A habit to be cultivated in this day and age. But sup-posing I had neglected to do so. You would have been running the very real risk of becoming pregnant.'

'I assumed you'd be careful,' she lied.

His lips twisted. 'A dangerous assumption indeed.' He seemed about to say something else, then apparently changed his mind. 'We will talk again later,' he declared.

He left her standing there, closing the outer door quietly behind him. 'A means of discovering the truth,' he'd said, but he didn't know the half of it, thought Gina hollowly. She hesitated to think what his reaction might be if he made *that* discovery.

With Ottavia watching for any sign that her suspicions had foundation, breakfast was an ordeal. Not that Lucius appeared to be aware of the interest his sister was taking in the pair of them. Men being men, he probably wouldn't be in the least bit fazed by it anyway, Gina reflected with a cynical edge.

Donata hadn't put in an appearance at all this morning. As no one had commented on her absence, she could only assume that it wasn't an unusual occurrence. She resolved to have a word with the girl at the first opportunity. It might not do any good, but at least she would have tried.

At dinner last night her mind had been on other matters; thinking about it now, she realised that if her father hadn't been killed, none of these people seated at table would have been here, while she herself might well have been. While she regretted never having known her natural father, it was the only thing she did regret. She'd certainly suffered no deprivation.

Contrary to Ottavia's prediction, the visit to the vineyards proved anything but boring. Lucius took her through the whole process from the harvesting of the grapes to the finished product in its distinctively shaped, dark blue bottle. Marcello left him to it.

Gina found the man a difficult character to fathom all round: part of the family, yet aloof from it too. She had tried once or twice to draw him into conversation, but his responses had been so monosyllabic she had given up.

She hadn't called home for several days, she recalled guiltily in the car returning to the villa. While her parents were accustomed to her living her own life in her own flat, they did like to stay in regular contact. So far as they knew, she was touring in Europe with no set itinerary. They would be starting to worry about her by now.

She had already decided that there was no question of

telling her mother about finding the Carandentes. Why rake up a past that for her was over and done with long ago? All she need say was that she'd had an accident with the car and was waiting for repairs to be completed.

Right now, the car was the least of her problems. She stole a glance at the man at her side, wishing she could tell what was really going on behind the impassive profile. There had been little indication of intimacy between them during the past few hours; she suspected he'd come to the conclusion that the affair was best left to die a natural death. He was probably right, but it still left an aching sense of loss.

'You still have to tell me why you pretended to be a woman of experience,' he said unexpectedly, as if sensing something of her thoughts.

'I pretended nothing,' Gina denied, gathering herself. 'You simply took it for granted.'

'You had the opportunity to correct me.'

'It would have made a difference?'

'It would have caused me hesitation, yes. Virginity is a precious commodity, not to be taken lightly. I have robbed your future husband of the gift.'

'I may not get married at all,' Gina replied with careful control. 'If I do, few Englishmen would expect an untouched bride—especially one my age, or more—so you needn't feel guilty about it.'

Lucius was silent for a moment or two. When he spoke again it was in neutral tones. 'So there is no reason why we should not continue to enjoy what we feel for each other?'

Every reason, came the thought, if she was to avoid even deeper involvement. 'None at all,' she heard herself saying regardless. 'You do realise that Ottavia already suspects

what's going on?' she added, blotting out the consequences. 'She was watching us like a hawk at breakfast.'

'It concerns you?' he asked.

'I thought it might concern you.'

The sculptured face took on a certain austerity. 'I am
not accountable to anyone but myself for my actions. If
Ottavia utters one word out of place to you, you will tell
me at once.'

If this morning was anything to go by, words were unnecessary, Gina could have told him. Something she was
going to have to put up with because it was beyond her to
forgo any further contact while she was here.

They had reached the villa. Lucius drew the car to a
stop, putting out a hand to detain her when she made an
automatic move to open the door.

'There are matters we must discuss,' he said with serious
expression. 'First and foremost—'

He broke off as Ottavia emerged from the villa, her face
like a thundercloud. She descended the steps to the open-
topped car, thrusting the long white envelope she was carrying at Gina, her eyes glittering with anger.

'What kind of trickery is this?' she demanded.

CHAPTER FIVE

GINA found her voice with an effort. 'You had no right to search my things!'

'What is it?' Lucius sounded bewildered. 'Ottavia?'

His sister lapsed into rapid Italian, from which Gina was able only to recognise the words Giovanni and *conjugali*. She didn't dare look at Lucius, sensing his growing confusion.

'I think this would be best discussed indoors,' he said at length, cutting through Ottavia's continuing tirade. He slid from his seat to come round and open Gina's door as she sat in frozen silence, eyes penetrating her defences. 'Come.'

She got out of the car and accompanied him up the steps into the villa, Ottavia following on behind. Lucius made for the library where they had first met, ushering both women through ahead of him, and closing the door.

'First,' he said in English, 'I will see for myself what is contained in the envelope.'

Ottavia handed it over, the look she gave Gina as she did so like a knife stab. 'A fake, of course,' she stated.

'I'm afraid it isn't,' Gina felt moved to retort. 'It's only too real.'

Lucius quelled her with a glance. Extracting the contents of the envelope, he studied first the photograph and then the licence, the muscles about his mouth tautening ominously as he read. Gina was unsurprised by the icy quality of his regard when he finally looked up.

'Who are you?' he demanded.

'Giovanni was my father,' she admitted.

'You told us your father was named Barsini,' Ottavia chimed in. 'Alexander Barsini!'

Gina lifted her shoulders in a helpless little shrug. 'I lied.'

'Why?' Lucius's voice was clipped, his whole demeanour the antithesis of the man she had known to date.

'It just seemed…easier, at the time.'

'Easier?'

'I wasn't sure you were the same Carandentes I was looking for.'

'You could have asked.'

She searched for the words to explain. 'I didn't feel able. I thought you might think I was looking for handouts. Money,' she translated, seeing his brows draw together afresh. 'All I wanted was to know who my father really was.'

'This is all lies!' Ottavia burst out. 'There was never any marriage!'

'Yes, there was!' Gina flashed. 'They fell in love at university. They didn't tell anyone about the wedding because they knew it wouldn't meet with approval—from either side. Giovanni was on his way home to tell his family when he was killed. My mother knew nothing of his background, except that he came from Vernici.'

Ottavia made a repudiative gesture. 'All lies!'

'Why would she make no effort to seek out his family herself?' asked Lucius.

Gina shrugged again. 'Perhaps because she was afraid of some claim being made to the baby she was carrying.'

'The child being yourself.'

'Yes.' She put up a somewhat shaky hand to her hair. 'This, and my mother's word, is the only real proof I have, of course.'

'You were conceived before the marriage took place.'

Her cheeks burned at the assumptive tone of the question. 'No, damn you!'

Lucius held up a staying hand. 'Anger alters nothing. If this licence is valid, you are a Carandente by right, regardless of the circumstances under which the marriage took place.'

'No!' Ottavia looked and sounded outraged. 'There can be no question of it!'

'You don't have to concern yourself,' Gina told her shortly. 'I want nothing from you.'

Lucius made an abrupt movement. 'Your requirements have no bearing on the matter. If you are Giovanni's child, you have more right to be here than we ourselves.'

'No!' Ottavia cried again.

Gina ignored her, her whole attention on Lucius. 'I'm not interested in rights. I told you, all I wanted was to know something about my father.'

The pause was lengthy, the eyes resting on her face, shorn of all expression. 'We will talk again when I have considered what is to be done,' he said.

Further protestations would be a waste of time and effort, Gina judged. For the moment, at any rate. Short of renouncing all claim to San Cotone in her favour, which was hardly likely, there was little enough he could do.

Ottavia burst into furious Italian again, answered by her brother in equally vehement tones. Gina left them to it. Clear of the room, she stood for an indecisive moment or two wondering what to do. With no transport available, she couldn't even ditch the whole problem and head for home. She had to stay and front it out: to somehow convince Lucius that she had no ulterior motives.

With memories of the night before hanging in the air, her bedroom proved no retreat. She had rinsed out the blood stain in the bathroom before going down to break-fast, with the intention of replacing the sheet on the bed when it was dry. It was gone now, the bed remade with fresh linen. Probably a daily happening, Gina thought wryly, wondering what conclusion the person given the task might have reached. One thing was certain: there would be no more nights like the last.

It still needed more than an hour to lunch. Not that food held any great appeal. She didn't give a damn about Ottavia, but she dreaded seeing Lucius again. And Donata. How was she likely to react? It was such a mess, and all her own fault. If only she'd left things alone!

Barely half an hour had passed when Lucius came to find her. He looked, Gina thought, as if weighty decisions had been made.

'We have much to discuss,' he stated.

'There's nothing *to* discuss,' she responded staunchly. 'I'm here under false pretences, and I'm sorry, but the way I feel is genuine enough. So far as I'm concerned, San Cotone is all yours. I want no part of it.'

Lucius eyed her with open scepticism. 'So why did you sleep with me last night?'

'Because I wanted to,' she said. 'Because you made me want to.'

'I was unaware of our relationship then. You were not.'

'We're hardly close relations.' Gina protested weakly. 'From what Cesare told me, we're no more than distant cousins.'

Lucius curled a lip. 'So you drew Cesare into your web too.'

'It wasn't like that. I wasn't sure I even had the right Carandente family until I spoke with him.'

'Which was when exactly?'

'Yesterday, when we were separated in Siena.'

'After which, you decided the time was right to surrender your virginity to me.'

'No!' Gina could see where this was leading. 'Not the way you mean. I felt…attraction towards you the moment we met, but I couldn't let myself give way to it until I was sure we weren't closely related. If Ottavia hadn't taken it on herself to search my room for some reason, you'd none of you ever been any the wiser.'

'You planned to leave the moment your car was ready for use again?'

'Yes.'

'Having spent several irresistible nights in my arms between times.' The scepticism had increased to searing proportions.

Gina passed the tip of her tongue over dry lips, trying to keep a level head. 'Having been there once, I daresay I might have succumbed to temptation again, but I'd still have gone when the time came. If I'd intended otherwise, why keep the photograph and licence concealed? I could hardly count on Ottavia coming across them.'

'How can I be sure of that? How can I be sure of anything where you are concerned?' Face set, eyes like black coals, Lucius wasn't giving an inch. 'Whatever your intentions, you leave me little choice. The obligation now is twofold.'

Gina gazed at him uncertainly. 'Obligation?'

'We must marry.'

Shock held her rigid for a several seconds, her mind blanked of all rational thought. 'That's quite ridiculous!' she managed at length.

'Other than relinquishing title to everything my family has known these past seventeen years, it is the only way I have of restoring honour.'

Gina searched her mind for the words needed to counteract the preposterous proposal, finding nothing of sufficient note. 'You said twofold?' she queried, playing for time to come up with *some*thing.

'A matter of honour once more.'

Blue eyes widened anew as his meaning went home. 'Because of last night? But it was my own choice.'

'It makes no difference. It is *my* duty to make reparation.' He was speaking now with a clipped quietness more telling than any amount of ranting and raving. 'Arrangements will be made immediately.'

'They most certainly will not!' Her voice had gathered strength, spurred by an anger that overwhelmed all other emotions. 'I've absolutely no desire to marry you! To marry anyone, if it comes to that!'

There was no hint of relief in his eyes at the pronouncement; if anything it served to firm their purpose even further. 'You would deny me the means of righting the wrong done to you?'

'You've done no wrong,' Gina insisted. 'This is the twenty-first century, for heaven's sake, not the Middle Ages!'

For all the impression she made she may as well have saved her breath. Lucius was already turning away. 'Arrangements will be made,' he repeated.

This was getting more and more incredible by the minute, thought Gina dazedly as he departed. Four days ago she had arrived in Vernici with just the one thought in mind. Never in a thousand years could she have imagined finding herself in a situation like this. She had a mental image of Ottavia's face when Lucius informed her of his intentions, and knew a sudden insane desire to laugh. Hysteria, she told herself, taking a firmer grip. Hardly surprising in the circumstances.

It wasn't going to happen, of course. She could hardly be forced into a marriage she didn't want. Lucius couldn't possibly want it himself. Not in any way that mattered.

She was still standing there in a daze when the door was flung open without ceremony. Ottavia looked ready to kill.

'You think yourself so clever!' she snapped. 'But I am not so easy to deceive! *You* are no Carandente!'

Much as she might wish at the moment that she had never come near the place, Gina took exception to the accusation. 'If I'm not,' she said with control, 'how would you explain the photograph and marriage licence?'

'You had them forged in the hope of making claim to San Cotone for yourself! It is a simple matter to join two photographs together!'

'And how would I have got hold of a photograph of Giovanni to do that?'

'It is quite possible that your mother and he were at the university at the same time. Possible too that they had a relationship, of which you were the result.' The last comment was on a contemptuous note that brought Gina's blood to near boiling point. 'But no Carandente would marry beneath their class!'

'Including yourself?' The words were out before Gina could stop them—immediately regretted.

Ottavia's olive skin had visibly paled. When she answered it was with venom. 'Marcello's ancestry is no less than my own. How dare you suggest otherwise!'

'How dare *you* come bursting in here accusing me of deception?' Gina retorted, abandoning the apology trembling on her lips. 'Like it or not, the marriage took place. If you don't believe the licence is real, you can have it checked quite easily. Not,' she added with deliberation, 'that your brother appears to doubt it.'

'Lucius is a fool!'

Gina raised a meaningful eyebrow. 'You're prepared to tell him that?'

The older woman looked as if she'd bitten into a bitter lemon. *'Vacca!'* she spat out.

Whatever the word meant, it was far from complimentary, Gina gathered from the tone. She checked the inclination to reply in kind, forcing a conciliatory note instead. 'There's no point in this. Ottavia. I no more want to be here than you want me to be.'

'Then, why come at all?'

Gina sat down on the bed, her legs too shaky to support her any longer. 'I already told you downstairs. I just wanted to trace my father's background. I had no idea of all this. Neither, I'm sure, did my mother.'

'You believe an English university within reach of the lower classes here?'

She had a point, Gina had to admit. The cost alone would have been prohibitive. 'I didn't consider that angle,' she confessed.

Ottavia still looked far from convinced. 'If it was so important to you to know Giovanni's background, then why have you waited so long?'

'I was fifteen before I knew anything at all about it. With school, university and then work, there hasn't been time to think about it before this. I'm between jobs at present, so I decided to take advantage of the break.' Gina spread her hands in a gesture meant to convey her own confusion. 'I never anticipated anything like this happening.'

'Including spending the night with a man you had known only a few days?'

Biting her lip, Gina said hollowly, 'He told you that?'

'That and more.' The antagonism was muted though by no means extinguished. 'My brother is a man to whom family honour is of great importance. To restore it he would make whatever sacrifice he considered necessary. You, he tells me, were a virgin before he unbeknowingly took you. In his view he would have no choice but to offer marriage, even without this other matter.'

'An offer I already turned down on both counts,' Gina stated, hating the thought of Ottavia being privy to the intimate detail, hating Lucius for making free with it. 'If you want to put a stop to it all, you can help me get away.'

Ottavia regarded her narrowly for a lengthy moment or two. When she did finally answer, it was on a rather more amenable note. 'Your own car has yet to be returned. If I drove you to Vernici you would still be without transport.'

'Then, drive me to Siena. If you can discover where my car is being repaired, there's a chance it might be ready.'

'And if it is not?'

'I'll deal with that if and when,' Gina answered with a confidence she was far from feeling. 'Just get me there.'

'If I did, it would have to be at night,' Ottavia said after a brief consideration. 'If we left after everyone is asleep, I could be back in my own bed before morning—able to deny any knowledge of your departure.'

'What about Marcello?' Gina asked.

'Marcello would say whatever was required.' Ottavia's voice had softened just a fraction. 'I believe I may have done you an injustice.'

As apologies went, it left something to be desired, but it was, Gina guessed, all she was going to get. She couldn't really blame the woman for feeling the way she did. She was hardly going to welcome the news that Giovanni Carandente had not after all died without issue.

'Think nothing of it,' she said.

If Ottavia noted any trace of satire, she gave no indication of it. 'That leaves us with the rest of today to get through. We must act naturally, the two of us, so that Lucius has no suspicion.'

Gina gave a brief, wry smile. 'Like enemies, you mean.'

There was no trace of regret in the other eyes. 'It should not be difficult.'

For her, perhaps not, Gina reflected. For herself, it was going to be the most difficult day she had ever spent. She still found it hard to believe it wasn't all some stupid dream she was going to waken from any minute. Except that dreams tended to have little consistency.

'You have fifteen minutes to prepare for lunch,' the other woman advised, glancing at her watch. 'I would suggest a change of clothing. The trousers you have on are stained. Tonight, we will meet at the garage compound. Two o'clock.'

She departed at that, leaving Gina to get stiffly to her feet to view herself in the cheval mirror. Her trousers were indeed stained, although the mark was small enough to go unnoticed by all but the most critical eyes. She exchanged them for a long skirt nevertheless. The grazes on her knee were healing fast but still needed covering. The memory of Lucius pressing his lips to the injury last night brought a painful tightness to her chest. He would take some forgetting for certain.

She turned her mind to the planned escape, forced to acknowledge the flaws. If, as was likely, her car wasn't ready, she could hardly abandon it and fly home, which meant she would have to sit it out in Siena hoping that Lucius would see fit to let the whole affair drop. In either case, she would probably have the repair bill to pay herself, with all the subsequent problems entailed in claiming on insurance, although that was a relatively minor detail in comparison.

*   *   *

It was three women to the one man at lunch, Marcello not in evidence. She found Donata already in possession of developments. Any ill-feeling over Cesare apparently forgotten for now, the girl seemed to view the whole situation in a totally different light from her sister.

'So you're actually a cousin!' she exclaimed. 'And soon to be a sister too!'

Blue eyes met impassive black ones across the width of the table. 'I'd doubt it,' Gina said levelly.

Donata looked from one to the other in sudden confusion. 'But Lucius told me—'

'It takes two to tango.' The flippancy was deliberative. 'I already said I wasn't interested.'

'Your lack of interest is duly noted,' he responded drily.

Donata looked even more confused. 'I don't understand. Did you not come to claim the inheritance that should have been yours?'

'No.'

'Then…why?'

'Curiosity.' Gina was tired of repeating the same thing over and over. 'It killed the cat.' She took pity on Donata's obvious incomprehension. 'Finding out who my father was seemed important once. I realise now it would have been better to let things alone.'

Lucius made an abrupt gesture. 'Too late for regrets. What must be must be.'

Catching Ottavia's eye, Gina refrained from comment. It was easier for now to let him believe her resigned to the prospect. By this time tomorrow she would be long gone. He might not be willing to acknowledge it, but he could only be relieved to find the onus removed.

She had little appetite for food, beautifully prepared and served though it was. Try as she might, she couldn't close out the memories evoked by every movement of the masculine hands. Last night those same hands had roved her whole body—had discovered her every intimate secret. It was going to be a long time before she could bring herself to make love with any other man.

He left them the moment the meal was over. To do what, he didn't say. Ottavia vanished too. Reluctant to be on her own with her thoughts, Gina was happy to settle for Donata's company on the terrace, even if it did involve answering more questions.

'It will be good to have a sister I can talk with,' declared the girl when her curiosity regarding Gina's life up to now was at last satisfied.

'Even one you believe was making up to Cesare only yesterday?' Gina asked steadily.

'I had reason then to be jealous,' she said. 'Now that you're to be married to Lucius, I have no more.'

Gina hesitated before making the attempt. 'I appreciate how you feel about Cesare, but he's almost twice your age.'

'Older men have so much more to offer than younger ones,' came the unconcerned reply. 'Cesare is not only the most handsome man I know, but the richest too. If I marry him I will be a marchioness.'

'Does everyone in this country have a title?' Gina queried only half in jest.

Donata took the question quite seriously. 'In our society there are few with no claim at all. Lucius is an exception in declining to use his own entitlement. You realise he won't allow you to take title yourself?'

'I wouldn't want to.' Gina could say that with truth.

'*Madre* is going to have such a surprise when she returns!' Donata declared. 'You'll be expected to produce a son to carry on the family name as soon as possible.'

One member of this family she wouldn't have to lie to,

thought Gina thankfully. 'Who is this Livia Marucchi she spoke of the other night?' she asked, surprising herself because she hadn't realised she even remembered the name.

'No one of any importance,' Donata assured her. 'Not now.'

'But Lucius has considered her as a prospective wife?'

'She would be suitable.'

Gina kept her tone casual. 'Is she attractive?'

'She is beautiful, but I have never seen Lucius look at her in the same way that he looks at you. I overheard him telling *Madre* once that he needed more than suitability in a wife. I know now that he meant he wanted someone who could also stir his blood.'

She'd done that all right, thought Gina ruefully. But it was still no basis for marriage.

The day wore on. Lucius was still absent when she went to change for the evening. Emerging from the bathroom some twenty minutes later to find him seated on one of the elegant chairs was a total shock. Motionless in the doorway, only too well aware of the emotions just the mere sight of that patrician face and lean, lithe body aroused, she took refuge in belligerence.

'What the devil do you think you're doing just walking in here?'

He studied her in turn before answering, eyes travelling her slender, shapely length in the short towelling robe all the way up from her bare toes to her flushed cheeks and sparking eyes, his expression unrevealing. 'The arrangements are made,' he said without apology.

'Like hell they are!' Hands clenched, Gina fought the small, treacherous part of her that leapt at the thought. 'There's no way I'm going to marry you!'

'You would betray your father by turning your back on the inheritance that should have been his before you?'

'That's utter rot!' she exclaimed.

'It is a fact,' he stated, still without raising his voice. 'Your mother and stepfather will, of course, be welcome to visit you.'

Gina felt hysteria welling up again. 'Will you get it through your head that it isn't going to happen,' she said through gritted teeth. 'So far as I'm concerned, your honour can go take a running jump!'

'It would be difficult, I think, for an abstract to perform such a feat.'

She made an abrupt gesture. 'There's nothing in the least bit funny about this!'

'I agree,' he said. 'It is a very serious matter.'

The pause was lengthy, the growing purposefulness in his regard increasing Gina's pulse rate by the second. Her heart leapt into her throat when he rose from the chair.

'It seems there is only one way to convince you,' he affirmed.

Gina's first thought as he moved towards her was to step back into the bathroom and close the door in his face. But there was no key, she recalled, no means of locking it at all, in fact.

'Whatever you have in mind, you can forget it!' she flung at him.

He paid no heed. Pulling her into his arms, he quietened her protests with his mouth, his hands sliding the length of her back to draw her up close against him.

Gina felt no sense of violation in the embrace; his hold on her was light enough to allow her to pull away from him again if she wanted to. Only, while her mind was saying one thing, her body was saying quite another, pressing instinctively closer to his heat and hardness. There was no doubting his desire for her—no denying her own for him. Conquering the urge to give way to it called for a strength of mind beyond her to summon right now. Did the whys and wherefores really matter? asked the fading voice of reason.

He lifted her without effort and carried her across to the bed. Gina made one last effort to drag herself out of it as he parted the towelling robe, but the feel of his lips at her breast was too much for her. Her legs parted on their own accord to his gently insistent urging, body arching as he found the tiny bud. All thought of resistance had flown. She wanted, needed, had to have the whole of him again!

The sensation when they came together was even more incredible than before: warm, vibrant velvet wrapped around a steel core. It was only on feeling the final hot rush of his release that she realised why he felt so different, and by then it was too late. Far, far too late!

'You did that purposely,' she whispered when he finally rolled away from her to sit up and adjust his clothing.

'True,' he agreed. 'I saw no other course.'

Gina sat up herself, pulling the robe jerkily around her. 'There's no certainty of pregnancy!'

'The chance alone should be enough,' he said.

She gazed at him in confounded silence for a moment or two, unable to come to terms with the sheer ruthlessness of his action. He met her gaze without a flicker of remorse.

'There are compensations for the loss of freedom for each of us.'

'If you mean, what we just did, I wouldn't let you near me again for a fortune!' she retorted.

A spark momentarily lit the dark eyes. 'I think you might be persuaded.'

He gave her no time to form a reply. Feeling totally at a loss, Gina made no move for several minutes after he'd left the room. Conception wasn't guaranteed, but it was a very real possibility. It would be another couple of weeks before she knew for certain.

One thing *was* certain, she told herself forcefully: whatever the outcome, there could be no marriage. She had planned to leave tonight, and leave she would. If she had to hang around in Siena waiting for her car to be ready, then so be it. Any attempt on Lucius's part to fetch her back would be dealt with by the police.

The question of what she would do if she did turn out to be pregnant she pushed to the back of her mind. There was nothing to be gained from dwelling on things that might not happen.

The others were already gathered in the *salotto* when she eventually geared herself into going down. Lucius poured the gin and lime she asked for and brought it across to where she sat, lifting a sardonic eyebrow in response to the black look she gave him. Little more than half an hour ago they had been together in the most intimate sense. It was hard, Gina thought hollowly, to equate the man who had held her then with the one who faced her now. They were two different people.

She refrained from drawing away when he took a seat at her side, although every instinct in her prompted the action. She could feel his body heat, smell his masculine scent. Casting around for some distraction, she caught Ottavia's meaningful glance, assuming it meant that tonight's venture was still very much on. Lucius would be bound to suspect his sister of having a hand in it, but that was her problem. She had enough to worry about on her own account.

If Donata sensed any untoward atmosphere, she showed no sign of it. Gina was sorry to deceive her—especially after what she had said earlier about having a sister she could talk with. She would need someone to turn to for solace when Cesare finally plucked up the guts to tell her where she stood with him, and she almost certainly wasn't going to get it from Ottavia.

As anticipated, it proved to be one of the longest, most fraught evenings Gina had ever spent. She stood it as long as she reasonably could before pleading tiredness. It was only on taking her leave that the possibility of Lucius planning a further visit to her room tonight occurred to her, although there was nothing in his attitude to suggest that he might have it in mind. Something else to be dealt with if and when, she thought wearily.

She felt safe enough, when no approach had been made by one-thirty, to get dressed again, having packed her suitcase earlier. Silence reigned when she left the bedroom. The suitcase was heavy. She regretted not ditching at least some of its contents; clothes could always be replaced. It was too late now, anyway. She would just have to manage. Once at the car there would be no problem.

There were lights still lit on the stairs and down in the hall, but no tell-tale strips beneath the doors. Glad of the flat pumps she had chosen as the most practical wear, Gina descended as quietly as she could.

Her elbow felt as though it was being pulled out of joint by the time she reached the hall. She set the suitcase down for a moment in order to ease the muscle. All this could have been hers, came the thought as she viewed the superb decor. This, and more. If only…

She stopped herself right there, unwilling to acknowledge the particular if only that had crossed her mind.

Traversing the whole of the ground floor to reach the rear of the house took longer than she had allowed for,

escaping via the bolted doors even longer. It was well gone
two when she finally reached the compound, to find
Ottavia waiting in a fever of impatience.

'I was beginning to think you had changed your mind,'
she snapped. She flung open the door of the car she had
already brought from the garage. 'We must go at once!'

Gina slung her suitcase in the back, then got into the
front passenger seat. It was too late now to change her
mind, even if she wanted to. And she didn't want to. Quite
definitely she didn't. There was nothing here for her.

The morning light did nothing to enhance the room's bare
white walls and sparse furnishings. Rising without reluctance from the bed that had afforded her little sleep, Gina
consoled herself with the thought that it was at least clean.

Best that she stay somewhere Lucius would never think
of looking for her, Ottavia had said on dropping her at the
door of the small backstreet hotel. The name and location
of the company handling the car repairs had completed her
contribution.

Gina hoped to be heading north before the day was
done, but until she could be sure she had to keep the room
on. Breakfast could wait. First and foremost she had to
check on the car.

Last night's desk clerk had shown a lively curiosity at
her late arrival. It was a relief to find him replaced by a
woman who called a taxi for her without showing any
interest whatsoever.

Ottavia had written the details down, enabling her to
simply show the paper to the driver with the minimum of
verbal exchange. The repair shop was no backstreet business. Not that Gina would have expected it. She was relieved to find the receptionist in the impressive front office
bilingual.

'My car is here for repair,' she advised. 'I'd like to know if it's ready yet, please.'

Armed with the registration number, the man brought up the details on computer screen, a frown creasing his brow as he studied them.

'There must be a mistake. This vehicle is to be returned to the Villa San Cotone when repairs are completed.'

'I'm staying there,' Gina said quickly. 'I thought I'd just check on it while I was in town.'

The frown gave way to apology as he once more scanned the screen. 'I'm afraid the work is not yet complete. A difficulty in obtaining a part.'

'How much longer might it take?' she asked, doing her best to mask the disappointment.

'If the part arrives today, the car will be ready tomorrow.'

If the part arrived today. Gina conquered the urge to demand some better assurance, doubting if it would do any good to get stroppy. Considering what she'd said about taking the chance while she was in town, it might look a little odd if she called in again tomorrow, but it was all she could do.

She spent the whole day exploring parts of the city not already seen, returning to the hotel to spend another night tossing and turning. By morning she was almost ready to abandon the car altogether rather than spend any more time hanging around.

She couldn't, of course. Cars didn't grow on trees. If it still wasn't ready, the best she could do was find somewhere a little more upmarket to stay until it was.

The hotel had neither lift nor porter to help with the transportation of luggage, but it was at least a little easier carrying her suitcase down three flights of stairs than it had been lugging it up. This was the very last time, she vowed, that she travelled with anything but a capsule wardrobe. Her arm sockets were never going to be the same again.

She reached the shabby lobby at last, with a sigh of relief. The same sullen woman who had been on duty yesterday watched without batting an eyelid as she dragged the case across to the desk.

'I'd like to check out please,' she said.

'*Non capisco,*' declared the receptionist without expression.

Gina gazed at her in rapidly mounting impatience. It had to be obvious to anyone but a total moron that she would hardly be touting a heavy bag all the way down here for any other purpose but to leave.

'*Terminare,*' she tried, reminding herself that she was the foreigner here. '*Quanto costa?*'

'*Adesso!*' ordered a crisp voice.

The woman went without haste to leaf through one of the card files on the desk, leaving Gina to turn and face the man at her back.

'How did you find me?' It was all she could think of to say.

Lucius regarded her dispassionately. 'Ottavia was persuaded to tell me where you were.'

'A few minutes more and I wouldn't have been.'

'So it appears. Fortunate then that I arrived when I did.'

He reached past her to take the slip from the woman behind the desk and give it a cursory glance. Gina made a small sound of protest as he took a billfold from an inner pocket of his jacket and extracted a clutch of notes, but he ignored her, tossing them down on the desk and bending to swing the suitcase up without effort.

'I have a car outside,' he said.

Gina had little choice but to go with him—for the moment, at any rate. The open-topped Lancia had already created a jam in the narrow, one-way street. Lucius turned a deaf ear to the irate shouts from those unable to proceed, slinging the suitcase in the boot and making sure Gina was secure in her seat before going round to get behind the wheel.

'I'm not coming back to San Cotone with you,' she stated as he put the vehicle into motion.

'How do you intend stopping me from taking you there?' he asked.

A good question, she acknowledged wryly. Jumping from a moving car was not to be recommended.

'You don't really want this,' she appealed. 'You can't possibly want it!'

'Do not,' he returned, 'tell me what I do or do not want. I make my own decisions.'

'A very bad one in this case.'

'The only one open to me.'

'But not to me.' Gina was doing her best to stay on top of her emotions. 'As I already told you, I want nothing from you.'

Expression unyielding, he said, 'You may have no choice in the matter.'

He meant the possibility of her being pregnant, Gina surmised. 'A chance I'm prepared to take,' she claimed with a great deal more certainty than she actually felt.

Lucius concentrated on extracting the car from a three-lane confluence before answering, 'You consider it no more than a chance?'

'No slur on your virility, but yes.'

The taunt made no visible impression. 'And if that chance became reality?'

She swallowed on the sudden lump in her throat. 'I'd deal with it.'

'In what manner?' His tone had sharpened.

She took his meaning immediately, with no need to consider her reply. 'It certainly wouldn't be abortion!'

'So you would bring up the child alone.'

'I wouldn't be alone. I'd have—' She broke off abruptly, shaking her head. 'There's no point in thinking about something that might not even happen! That definitely *wouldn't* be happening if you hadn't…done what you did!'

'As you yourself were unprotected the first time, it may still have happened,' came the brusque reply. 'There is no such thing as a hundred per cent guarantee.'

There was a pause while he negotiated a busy junction. When he spoke again it was on a moderated note. 'I make no excuses for my actions. It was wrong of me. I have no right to stop you from leaving, if that is what you wish, but you must promise me one thing.'

Gina swallowed again on the same lump. 'What?'

'That if there is to be a child, you will allow me to take responsibility for the welfare.' He winged a swift glance when she failed to reply right away, mouth tautening anew. 'On this I *must* insist.'

'All right.' It was the only reply she could make in the circumstances. Eyes fixed on the traffic ahead, she added tonelessly, 'So where now?'

'We go to pick up your car,' he said. 'The readiness was confirmed to me late yesterday afternoon. You can be on your way home before noon.'

Gina felt her chest constrict. 'You intended that all along?' she got out.

'Only if you made it quite clear to me that you have no interest in becoming my wife, whatever the incentive.' His tone was as flat as hers. 'My conscience must, it seems, remain unappeased.'

'You don't have anything to feel guilty about,' she re-iterated. 'If I'd left well alone, you'd never have known about me.'

'But you did come, and I do know. And I must learn to live with the knowledge that San Cotone is mine only by default.'

Gina had no reply to that. None, at any rate, that would help him come to terms with the situation. She should be feeling relieved that he'd seen sense regarding the marriage idea, but all she did feel was despondency.

Washed and gleaming, the Fiat looked fresh from the showroom. Lucius hoisted Gina's suitcase into the boot, and locked it, handing over the keys without further delay.

'You have your route planned?' he asked.

'I'll just reverse the one I took coming down.' She hesitated, searching the incisive features, reluctant now that the moment was here to make the final move. 'I'm really sorry for putting you in this position.'

The dark eyes concealed whatever thoughts were going on behind them. 'I am the one who should apologise for attempting to force you into a union that would benefit only myself. Just remember your promise.'

She murmured some assurance, unwilling to acknowledge the possibility that she might be called upon to keep her word. With no more reason to linger, she got into the car and started the engine, taking a moment to fasten her seat belt before releasing the handbrake. The last glimpse she had of Lucius was through the driving mirror as she turned out onto the road: an image that was to stay with her throughout the long journey home.

CHAPTER SIX

COMING three days after starting her new job, the evidence that she wasn't pregnant should have proved a source of relief not despondency. Gina contemplated putting Lucius's mind at rest on that front at least, but shrank from making contact again.

The one visit she had paid home since her return from the European trip had been difficult. Her parents had naturally wanted to hear all about it. If she had turned out to be pregnant they would have had to know the truth, of course, but with that particular pressure removed there was no need for them to know anything.

She left it till the end of the month before making another trip, travelling up on the Friday evening in order to have a lengthier stay. Her mother's greeting was unusually subdued.

'I suppose you have to know sometime,' she said. 'Hayes and Harlow have cancelled their contract.' She made a wry gesture. 'Turning over the whole production line to one company was a big mistake.'

With Redman's not the only one to make it, Gina reflected. Not that knowing it was any solace. She had entertained doubts herself over the contract set up five years ago, but hadn't felt qualified at the time to express them. Now her worst fears had been realised.

'What's the outlook?' she asked, already knowing the answer.

'Bankruptcy, if substantial new orders aren't forthcom-

ing inside the next month or so,' Beth confirmed. 'John
borrowed to the limit again to renew the machinery last
year. The bank will foreclose if he can't prove his viability.
We could lose the house too.'

Gina let out her breath on a faint sigh. It was worse
even than she had imagined. 'Where's Dad now?'

'In the study, trying to make the figures add up differently. He's spent the whole week looking for new business.
Without very much success, I'm afraid.'

Not really to be wondered at after five years, Gina
thought. Even if orders could be gleaned it wouldn't help
the immediate problems. What was needed was an injec-
tion of capital to keep things going until the company was
in profit again—fortune allowing.

Only how? She could probably manage to scrape ten
thousand or so together, but it was going to take a great
deal more than that.

'Is it all right if I go in to him?' she asked, shying away
from the thought that sneaked into mind.

'He'll welcome the interruption,' her mother assured
her. 'He's very depressed, although he tries hard not to
show it.'

Gina didn't wonder. It would be very hard to be anything else but depressed over a situation like this one.

She left her mother in the sitting room, and went through
to the front of the house where the study was. Compared
to San Cotone, a four-bed detached set in a bare acre was
no big deal, but she had spent an idyllic childhood here,
and still regarded it as home.

San Cotone. She closed her mind to the images—and to
the suggestion still hovering. There had to be some other
way!

Her tap on the door elicited no response. She opened it
to find her father seated at his paper-strewn desk under the

window with his head in his hands and a look of defeat about his bowed shoulders.

'Hallo, sweetheart!' he said, making a visible effort to lift his mood along with his head. 'When did you get in?'

'About twenty minutes ago,' Gina confirmed. 'You didn't hear the car?'

'I didn't notice. How are things with you?'

'Fine.' She went on impulse to slide her arms about his neck and press a kiss to the bald spot developing at his crown. 'Mom told me about H. and H. I'm so sorry.'

'My own fault for putting my faith in long-term assurances,' he said. 'I'm just sorry that your mother has to suffer the consequences too. It will break her heart to lose the house. She's put so much into it over the years.'

'Will it really come to that?' Gina asked.

'Unless a miracle happens, very probably. I've managed to secure a couple of one-off orders, but it takes time to build up a reliable customer list again, and time is in pretty short supply. I'll have to start laying people off, which means I'm not going to be in a position to accept substantial work if and when it becomes available.' He broke off, shaking his head in self-recrimination. 'I shouldn't be burdening you with it all!'

'Who else but family?' She paused, unable this time to turn a deaf ear to the inner voice. 'I might be able to provide some time.'

Her father gave a faint smile. 'It's a nice offer, darling, only the amount I'd need to have any chance at all of sticking it out would be more than you could possibly hope to raise.'

'I'm not talking about raising a loan,' she said. 'It would be more of an investment.'

His brow puckered. 'Just who do you think would be

prepared to invest in a company that's so close to going to the wall?'

'Someone I recently met might.' Gina straightened purposefully. 'I'll need to make a phone call. In private, if you don't mind.'

John Redman made no protest as she left the room. She went upstairs to use the extension in the master bedroom. It would be around ten-thirty Italian time, which would probably mean dragging Lucius away from the dinner table, but it had to be now, before she had time to think too deeply about it.

It took the international operator several minutes to make the connection. Guido answered, his voice instantly recognisable.

'It's Signorina Redman,' Gina said slowly and clearly. 'I want to speak with Signor Carandente. *Urgente*,' she tagged on.

Whatever the man's thoughts, he made no protest. Gina drew an unsteady breath when the familiar, sensual voice came on the line bare moments later.

'Gina? Where are you?'

'At my parents' home.' She hurried on before he could comment. 'I'm in need of help.'

There was a pause before he answered. 'Of what kind?'

'Money.' She made the statement deliberately bald. 'What else?'

'What else indeed?' His tone had hardened. 'For what reason do you need money?'

'Not what you're thinking,' she denied. 'My father's business is under threat of bankruptcy. Given a little time he can bring it round—' she hoped that was true '—but he doesn't have the capital available to see him through. I thought you might care to make an investment on the strength of our...relationship.'

The pause this time was even lengthier. 'And the sum in question?' he said at last.

'I'm not sure,' she confessed, having focused only on the actual request up to now. 'You'd have to speak to my father about that.'

'He knows you are making this call?'

'No. As a matter of fact, he doesn't even know you exist yet. Neither does my mother. I only found out about this whole mess half an hour or so ago. If you're going to say no,' she burst out, 'just say it!'

'My answer will very much depend on the return offered,' he said. 'I think it a subject best discussed in person. I can be with you by tomorrow afternoon. That will give you a whole night and morning to explain to your parents who exactly I am.'

So what had she expected? Gina asked herself hollowly: that he'd simply write out a cheque and post it to her? The last thing she wanted was to see him again, but she didn't have a great deal of choice if she was to secure the rescue package her father so desperately needed.

'I suppose,' she said, 'I'd better tell you where to come.'

'No need,' came the smooth return. 'I had both you and your family traced.'

'How?' she asked blankly.

'The information you gave me when you were here was sufficient. I had no trust in your promise.' He paused briefly. 'You must know by now.'

'I'm not pregnant,' she said.

The silence was weighty. 'Until tomorrow, then,' he said at length.

Gina replaced the receiver, wondering whether it was relief or disappointment she had sensed in his voice. His failure would probably weigh heaviest with him, she decided with irony. Men took such pride in their virility.

She had the task now of explaining things to her parents. Of the two of them, it was going to come as the greatest shock to her father, who wasn't even aware that she knew about Giovanni Carandente.

It seemed best to put her mother in the picture first. She found her in the kitchen, making coffee. Beth listened in stunned silence to the carefully edited story.

'I never realised quite how deeply you felt about it all,' she confessed ruefully. 'I knew Giovanni came from a good background, but he never said very much about his home life.' She paused, her brow puckering as she went over the detail in her mind again. 'What I can't understand is what interest this Lucius could possibly have in John's business problems.'

'He feels he owes me for what should by rights be mine.' That much Gina could say with truth.

'Which very likely would have been yours if I'd had the courage to go and find his family myself.'

'And robbed us both of the life we've had here with Dad. I wouldn't exchange that for *any* fortune!'

'Bless you,' Beth responded gratefully. She shook her head. 'It's still hard to take in. Lucius Carandente sounds a very upright and principled man.'

Gina wondered if she would say the same of the man who had made purposely unprotected love to her.

'He'll be relieved to unload some of the burden,' she said. 'I'm only sorry that Dad has to know where the money's coming from.'

Beth sighed. 'I shouldn't have asked you to keep it from him that you knew about Giovanni in the first place. He'll be reluctant to accept help from such a source, but he can hardly afford to turn it down.' She made a decisive movement. 'I'll tell him the story myself if you don't mind.'

Gina didn't mind at all. It had been difficult enough

telling it the once. The bits she had left out weighed
heavily on her mind, but at least she didn't have pregnancy
to add to the score.

Lucius arrived as promised the following afternoon, in a
car hired from the airport. Opening the door to him, Gina
composed her features into what she hoped was an inscru-
table expression, the tightness in her chest increasing pain-
fully on sight of the arresting face. He was wearing a superbly tailored suit in mid blue, with a darker toned shirt
and tie, the whole effect stunning.

'Good journey?' she asked huskily.

'As to be expected,' he said. He dropped the suitcase
he was carrying on the floor next to the umbrella stand,
studying her narrowly. 'You look drained. Were you telling me the truth last night?'

'Yes,' she confirmed. 'My parents are waiting to meet
you in the drawing room, but perhaps you'd like to go up
to your room first?'

The expression that flickered across the dark eyes was
come and gone too swiftly for analysis. He shook his head.
'I see no reason to delay matters.'

Gina had expected no less. He wouldn't want to be here
any longer than absolutely necessary. She paused with her
hand on the doorknob to say levelly, 'You realise, of
course, that there'll be little chance of capital repayment?
The best Dad could offer is a partnership.'

The lean features acquired a sudden austerity. 'There
will be no question of either. Whatever sum I invest, it
can only be a small part of your entitlement.'

Both Beth and John Redman came to their feet as they
entered the room, the former advancing with a somewhat
strained smile.

'It's so good of you to come all this way, Signor Carandente.'

'The very least I could do,' he assured her. He took the hand she offered in greeting and raised it briefly to his lips, his own smile as he lowered it again totally at ease. 'Please call me Lucius.'

From her expression, her mother was as bowled over by him as she herself had been on first acquaintance, Gina thought. Shades of Giovanni, perhaps.

John Redman had also come forward, his reticence apparent from the tension in his jaw line. 'It's been shock on shock this last couple of days,' he said. 'I hope you'll forgive me if I seem a bit dazed by it all.'

'I understand your feelings,' Lucius assured him, shaking hands. 'I felt the same sense of shock on first discovering the truth. Gina tells me you have business problems. Perhaps we might discuss them together.'

Meaning in private, Gina assumed. She opened her mouth to dispute the idea, closing it again on catching her mother's eye. She was right, of course. This was between the two men now.

'Have you had lunch?' she asked.

'On the flight,' Lucius confirmed. 'But I would welcome a coffee while your father and I talk.'

'I'll bring it through,' she said. 'Dad?'

'I'll have the same, please.' He was obviously finding it difficult to adjust to the younger man's direct approach. 'If you'd like to come to the study, I can show you the books.'

Lucius inclined his head. 'That would be a good start.'

Gina looked at him sharply, but there was nothing in his expression to suggest sarcasm. He wouldn't stoop that low, anyway, she assured herself. He was here to right what he considered a wrong in any way that he could.

She gave her mother a faint smile as the two men left the room. 'And that, as they say, is that! Or it will be by the time he's finished. I'll go make the coffee.'

They were already well into it when she took the tray through some ten minutes later. Neither man paid her more than a passing attention, leaving her feeling distinctly miffed. She, after all, was the catalyst in all this.

It was well over an hour before they emerged from the study. Her father, Gina thought, looked considerably better than he had earlier, if not altogether his usual self.

'Everything okay?' she asked.

Lucius answered for them both. 'It will be. If you would show me where I am to sleep, I would like to change into something a little more casual.'

'Of course,' she said.

She made an attempt to pick up his suitcase from the hall, to find it taken firmly from her hand. 'I will do my own carrying,' he declared. 'Just lead the way.'

Gina did so, vibrantly conscious of his presence at her back as they mounted the stairs. So far he had shown no inclination to touch her in any fashion at all. Hopefully, he would continue to observe the same rule.

She was lying through her teeth, and she knew it. She *ached* for him to touch her! Had done since the moment she'd laid eyes on him again. And not just touch either. She wanted him the way she had always wanted him.

The guest bedroom was next door to the one still regarded as hers. 'No *en suite* bathroom, I'm afraid,' she said with forced lightness, pausing in the doorway as Lucius moved forward to swing his suitcase up onto the blanket chest at the foot of the double bed. 'It's right opposite though, and there is a shower, if you want one.'

'I am sure I shall be very comfortable.' He looked back

to where she stood, raising an ironic eyebrow. 'You fear my actions?'

Not so much his as her own, she could have told him. 'Not in the least,' she denied. 'I just want to say how much I appreciate what you're doing. If there had been any other way...'

'You would have taken it.' The pause was brief, his expression resolute. 'There is a condition attached.'

Gina gazed at him in slowly dawning realisation, heart beginning an irregular tattoo against her ribcage. 'You're saying you'll only advance the money to my father if I agree to marry you?'

There was no element of apology in his regard. 'Exactly that. It is the only course I have left to me.'

'You're putting me in an impossible position!' she protested thickly.

'You would prefer to see your father made insolvent?' He gave her no time to answer, jaw firming afresh. 'Nothing you can say or do will change my mind this time. I will know no peace until your rights are restored.'

He meant it, she knew. Throat constricting, Gina closed the door on him, leaning against the jamb for a moment to try and calm herself down. None of this would be happening, she thought wretchedly, if she'd left well alone to start with!

Except that there'd be no rescue package for Redman's at all if she had, of course. If nothing else, she could be thankful for that.

She found her mother in the kitchen preparing a special dinner in celebration.

'We have a lot to be thankful for,' Beth acknowledged. 'Although John is still having trouble coming to terms. Talk to him, will you?'

No amount of talking could alter the fact that he was

having to rely on a member of her real father's family for aid, Gina reflected, but she kept the thought to herself. There was a whole lot she was keeping to herself. For as long as she could, at any rate.

The guest room door was closed when she went up for a shower and change of clothing, with no sound of movement from within. She wondered if Lucius had seen fit to inform his family of his renewed intentions. Their reactions if he had were fairly predictable. While Donata might be willing to accept it, Ottavia certainly wouldn't. Neither could his mother be expected to look on the union with any favour.

The whole thing was impossible, she thought desperately. One way or another, Lucius had to be made to see sense!

In her own room, she undressed and put on a cotton wrap, laying out clean underwear and a blue silk tunic in readiness for her return. There was still no sound from Lucius when she got to the bathroom. She flicked the catch on the door handle before sliding out of the wrap and starting the water running in the cabinet.

Soothed by the warm flow, she lingered longer than usual. The shock when Lucius opened the cabinet door and stepped inside with her rendered her speechless for several vital seconds.

He wasted no breath on words himself, turning off the water and sliding a hand beneath the dripping black mass of her hair to draw her to him. Her protest died beneath the pressure of his lips, her response instantaneous and uncontrollable. She tremored at the feel of him, nipples peaking as they rubbed against his chest hair, thighs parting to the lordly demand—no thought in mind other than the breathtaking sensation when he lifted her to receive him.

She stood with eyes closed when he finally set her down again, trying to regain control of herself.

'The door was locked,' she got out. 'How—?'

'The door was not locked,' Lucius denied softly. 'Although it is now. I came to take a shower myself, not realising you were already here.'

'You could have left again.'

'I could,' he agreed. 'But the flesh was weak. As was your own.'

She opened her eyes to view the water-beaded face, her body reacting even now to his closeness. 'Don't do it,' she pleaded. 'Don't force me into marrying you!'

'I have no choice,' he said. 'There is no other way.'

He stepped from the cubicle, unself-conscious in his nudity as he seized a towel and held it up for her, expression relentless. 'You have had your shower. I still need mine.'

Gina took the towel from him and wrapped it about herself before stepping from the cubicle. He took her place, closing the door between them before turning on the water flow again, body clearly outlined through the glass.

The short silk robe tossed carelessly on the floor was mute testimony to his claim, but she didn't believe for a moment that what had just happened between them was any spur-of-the-moment idea. His failure to impregnate her struck right at the heart of his manhood. Other matters apart, he would know no rest until he proved himself.

He was still showering when she left the bathroom, having made certain that neither of her parents were in the vicinity first. If she couldn't convince Lucius to abandon his stance they were in for another shock anyway, but she would hate them to know just how far things had already gone.

Beth had prepared a meal fit for a king, though Gina scarcely tasted any of it. Dressed casually now in trousers and light cotton sweater, Lucius appeared completely at ease with himself. When he made the announcement over coffee it took her every ounce of self-control she possessed to conceal her reactions.

John Redman was the first to recover his power of speech. 'Isn't this a little sudden?' he said with admirable restraint. 'You barely know one another!'

'It is not without precedent,' Lucius answered smoothly. 'History often repeats itself.'

The intimation was lost on neither one of the older couple. Seeing the expression that flickered across her mother's face, Gina could have choked at the cause of it.

'Why didn't you tell us about this yesterday?' asked her father. 'You gave no indication.'

'It hardly seemed the right time,' she prevaricated. 'You had too much on your mind already.'

'Matters which will be taken care of tomorrow,' said Lucius.

There was discomfiture in the older man's response. 'Grateful as I am for what you're doing, I can't pretend to be happy about it.'

'Your daughter is *my* only concern,' Lucius returned. 'San Cotone is where she belongs.'

'Just how soon are you planning on making the wedding?' asked Beth with constraint. 'It isn't something that can be arranged overnight.'

'We would prefer an informal ceremony,' Lucius answered, once again before Gina could speak—had she had a reply ready anyway. 'And as soon as is possible.'

'What about your family? They'll surely want to attend?'

This time Gina got in first. 'I'd doubt it. We don't have their approval.'

'That applies only to my elder sister,' Lucius advised calmly. 'My mother and younger sister are very much in approval. My mother unfortunately broke a bone in her foot, so she would find it difficult to travel. And Donata would be reluctant to come alone.'

Like hell she would! Gina thought. What he meant was she wouldn't be offered the chance.

'I'm sorry to hear about your mother's accident,' she said, not believing a word of it. 'How did it happen?'

'She fell getting out of the car on her return from Umbria,' he answered without batting an eyelid. 'She has it in a plaster cast.'

'Poor Cornelia!' Gina laid on the sympathy with a ladle. 'She must hate being incapacitated!'

There was a growing spark in the dark eyes, but his tone remained easy. 'Very much so.' He glanced over to the window where the evening sun slanted through. 'Perhaps we might take a walk in the garden while the light lasts?'

'Yes, do,' Beth urged, obviously desperate for breathing space. 'It's at its best right now.'

Hardly to be compared with what he was used to, Gina reflected, but that wasn't the point of the exercise.

It was pleasantly warm outside, the flower beds aglow with colour, the lawns immaculate as always.

'This all your stepfather's work?' Lucius asked.

'His and my mother's,' Gina confirmed. 'I never think of him as my stepfather,' she added. 'He gave me his name.'

'Soon to be exchanged for the one to which you were always entitled.'

She slanted a glance at the hard-edged profile outlined

against the setting sun, unable to deny the stirring deep inside her at the thought of being married to this man. A bare month ago she hadn't even known of his existence.

'There's still time to change your mind,' she said.

He turned his head to look at her, expression difficult to decipher. 'I already told you, I have no intention of changing my mind. Tomorrow, after your father's affairs are dealt with, we make the arrangements.'

'Is it really necessary to do it in such a hurry?'

'In the possible circumstances, yes.' Lucius shook his head as she started to speak. 'Whether or not, it makes no difference.'

'It does to me.' Gina made every effort to keep her tone level. 'I have a job for one thing. I can't just walk out on it.'

The shrug was eloquent. 'The matter will be taken care of.'

'There's a limit to the things money can buy!' she flashed, losing what tenuous control she still possessed. 'There are women, I'm sure, who would think a loveless marriage was no big deal in such circumstances, but I'm not one of them!'

Something flickered deep down in the dark eyes. 'We are hardly indifferent towards each other.'

'I'm not talking about sex! You could get that anywhere. We both could.'

This time there was no mistaking the expression in his eyes. 'There will be no other man in your life,' he stated brusquely. 'I will make sure of that!'

Gina lifted her chin. 'And no other woman in yours?'

'Of course.'

She didn't believe him for a moment. He might desire her now but, with nothing else to sustain it, the appetite would wither. The same, she imagined, for herself—eventually.

'It's impossible!' she burst out desperately. 'Please, Lucius, don't carry this through!'

'I have no choice,' he repeated. 'We neither of us have a choice. As to sex not being enough...' his lips slanted with slow sensuality '...then we must make it so.'

'Not here,' Gina whispered as he drew her to him. 'It isn't even dark yet!'

He stilled her protests with a kiss so passionate it blotted out everything but the feel of it. He slid his hands into the thickness of her hair to caress the tender skin behind her ears with his fingertips, starting a burn that spread rapidly throughout her body. Gina moved instinctively closer to him, the need to be closer still overwhelming in its force. The desolation when he put her suddenly and firmly away from him was almost too much to bear.

'Is love really so vital to you?' he asked softly. 'Can you not be content with what I make you feel?'

Contentment was the last thing she felt at the moment, she could have told him, fighting to contain the emotions coursing through her. He had her hog-tied in every direction.

'It seems I have to be,' she got out.

'There will be other compensations,' he said.

He meant motherhood, Gina surmised. She felt a sudden, spreading warmth at the thought. Marriage and children might not be every woman's ultimate aim in life, but it held infinitely more appeal for her than the career she had been pursuing so half-heartedly these last years, she had to admit.

'I suppose I owe it to Giovanni,' she murmured, giving way to the growing urge, and saw the unreadable expression flicker once more in his eyes.

'I also.' For a brief moment as he studied her he seemed about to say something else, then he made an abrupt movement. 'It grows cool. We should return to the house.'

By English standards it was a balmy evening, but the temperature was a whole lot lower than it would be in Tuscany right now, Gina knew. She would be a liar if she tried to pretend that the idea of living in such surroundings had no bearing. If only...

She cut the thought off before it could come to fruition.

It was a fraught evening all round, although the older couple did their best to put a good face on things. Most of all, Gina regretted the deception being practised on them, but knew her father would rather the business went down than allow her to marry Lucius against her will. Which it wasn't anyway. Not any more.

All the same, it took everything she had to restrain herself when Lucius suggested they visit the register office to make the necessary arrangements first thing on Monday.

'I have business in Rome on the seventh,' he said. 'We can continue from there to wherever you would like to spend the following days.'

Gina eyed him uncertainly. 'You mean a honeymoon?'

'Of course.' His smile was devoid of mockery. 'All newlyweds have need of a little time alone together.'

'The seventh is little more than a week away,' Beth pointed out. 'Isn't that rushing things a bit too much?'

Lucius turned the smile her way. 'Had it not been for Gina's insistence on returning to England to break the news to you in person, the wedding would have taken place three weeks ago—with your attendance, of course. Now that I am here myself, there seems no further reason to delay.'

'There's your job,' John Redman appealed to Gina. 'You can't just up and leave!'

'If some financial adjustment has to be made, it will be done,' Lucius answered before she could respond.

'But what about your career?' the older man insisted. 'The work you put in to get where you are? Are you going to throw all that away?'

Gina conjured a smile of her own. 'A career isn't everything, Dad.'

He made a resigned gesture. 'If that's the way you see it, there's nothing more to say.'

'Just so long as you're happy,' said Beth.

'I am.' Gina could only hope she sounded confident of it. She caught Lucius's eye, wishing she could tell what was really going on in that arrogant dark head of his. 'We both are.'

'Very much so,' he agreed. 'Your daughter will want for nothing, I assure you. I will take the greatest care of her always. As soon as you have your business affairs under control, you must come and visit with us.'

The thought must have crossed Beth's mind that, had Giovanni not been killed, San Cotone could well have been her own home, but her response gave no hint of it. 'We'll look forward to that.'

She stirred herself, looking at Gina with obvious intent. 'Come and help me with coffee.'

'If all this was arranged while you were over there, why didn't you tell us as soon as you got back?' she asked when the two of them were alone together.

Gina made a wry face. 'It was difficult to find a way. Especially when I hadn't even told you I was planning to look the Carandentes up in the first place. I was going to come clean about the whole thing this weekend anyway. It just worked out a little differently.'

'It's all happened so fast!' her mother exclaimed. 'You can't have known Lucius more than a few days!'

'How long did it take you to know how you felt about Giovanni?' Gina asked softly.

It was Beth's turn to pull a wry face. 'Point taken. I was head over heels on first sight of him. He was very much like Lucius,' she added reminiscently. 'Not all that much in looks, perhaps, but definitely in manner. He knew exactly what he wanted, and wouldn't take no for an answer.' She gave a little laugh, her colour rising. 'As you might have gathered. At least you're not…' She broke off, eyes asking the unvoiced question.

Gina shook her head. After this afternoon, she couldn't be wholly sure, but that was something to be thought about later.

'But you do love him? I mean, you're not marrying him for…other reasons?'

'Money, you mean?' Gina shook her head again, able to say that much with total truth. 'I don't feel any sense of being done down that way. There's no certainty that San Cotone would ever have been mine even if Giovanni had lived.'

'But you told me yesterday that Lucius considered himself under obligation to you.'

'That's the kind of man he is.' Gina kept her tone light. 'Nothing to do with the way we feel about each other. One look was enough for us both, just the way you said.'

'As *he* said, history repeats itself.' Her mother's eyes were misty. 'I'm sure you'll have a wonderful life together!'

Gina made the appropriate response, hoping she was right. Love could grow between two people, she supposed. Of a kind, at any rate. If she wasn't pregnant already, it was odds on that she would be before too long. Lucius needed a son if the Carandente name was to survive. Children could cement a shaky marriage.

Contrary to her expectations, Lucius made no attempt to invade her room that night. Considering what had happened in the shower earlier, it was a bit late for courteous gestures on the grounds of this being her parents' home, leaving her to conclude that his desire for her was far from irresistible. It was a long time before sleep overcame the hunger churning her own insides.

CHAPTER SEVEN

EVENTS moved quickly over the following week. With Redman's safeguarded, and the wedding booked for the sixth, it left just five days in which to settle personal affairs. The company Gina worked for proved surprisingly amenable to her leaving at a moment's notice—causing her to suspect that Lucius had already made an approach behind her back. Certainly, his offer of six months' rent on the flat in lieu of notice settled any protests her landlord might have made.

Apart from her clothes and a few bits and pieces, there was nothing she wanted. Definitely nothing she needed, considering where she was going to be living. She still found it difficult to take in that her whole life could change so radically in the space of a few weeks.

The one London friend she considered close enough to be put in the picture viewed the whole situation from a purely romantic aspect. A fairy tale come true, was her summing up.

'Drop-dead gorgeous, *and* superrich!' she commented when Lucius left the two of them alone for few minutes in the restaurant where they'd met for lunch. 'What more could anyone want!'

Some deeper emotion than duty alone, perhaps, thought Gina wryly. They had made love at the flat last night— she felt her stomach muscles contract at the very memory of it—but she was no closer to knowing the man within.

* * *

'I'm leaving my whole life behind,' she said in the car on the way back north that afternoon. 'Family, friends, career…'

'You can visit family and friends whenever you wish to,' Lucius answered steadily. 'Or have them visit you. If you fear becoming bored with no job of work to attend, you might like to join Marcello in the winery offices on occasion.'

Gina stole a glance at the clean-cut profile, suspecting satire. 'Oh, I'm sure he'd go for that!'

'It would not be his place to refuse.'

She hesitated before voicing the thought. 'It seems odd that your sister's husband should work for the company at all. Especially when she told me he shares the same kind of ancestry as the Carandentes.'

'His forebears held title, yes,' Lucius agreed. 'Unfortunately, he made some extremely bad investments after he and Ottavia were married, and lost what was left of the family fortune—including their home. He became comptroller as a means of salvaging his pride on being forced to take up residence at San Cotone.'

'I see.' Gina felt a pang of sympathy for the man. 'Well, I daresay I'll find plenty to occupy me without forcing myself on him. It's going to be bad enough as it is.'

'Ottavia will not be making life difficult for you,' Lucius stated authoritatively.

Maybe not while he was around, came the thought. She shrugged it off. There were far more important things to think about.

The wedding day was hot and sunny, the ceremony brief. Gina wore a cream dress a few shades lighter than Lucius's suit, her wide-brimmed coral hat a last-minute impulse buy she was only too glad to abandon on changing into something a little more practical for the journey to Rome.

Their flight to Heathrow was at a quarter to four, with a connection at five-thirty. They took their leave of her parents at the house. Whatever reservations John Redman might still harbour deep down, he had given the two of them his wholehearted support this past week. Gina turned her face resolutely forward as the car pulled away. She was a Carandente in name now, with a whole new life to live. There was no going back.

The domestic flight was uneventful, the connection on time, landing in Rome just before nine. The hotel where they were to spend the next two nights before travelling south to Capri was set in a square off the Via Claudia, its interior decor a symphony in gilt and crystal and silk-screened walls. Their suite was sheer luxury.

No more so than San Cotone, Gina reflected, taking it in. Something she was going to have to get used to—though hopefully never become complacent about.

'Tired?' asked Lucius softly as she turned from the window with its superb views over the illuminated city.

If she had been, the look in the dark eyes would have roused her. Make the most of it while it lasted, she told herself.

He undressed her slowly, sensually, somehow managing to rid himself of his own clothing at the same time. The smooth olive skin felt wonderful, the muscle rippling beneath as she traced a passage down the length of his body with her fingertips to claim the vibrant manhood. His mouth was a flame searing her breast, the curl of his tongue about her tingling nipple a pleasure close to pain.

He turned back the silk covers on the wide bed before lowering her to it, his lips creating mayhem in their intimate seeking. Gina writhed beneath him in an onslaught of sensation. She could live without love, came her last, fading thought as he slid inside her, but she couldn't live without this. Not ever!

Lucius was gone from the bed when she awoke to morning light. He came through from the sitting room already fully dressed in a formal dark blue suit, bending to press a brief kiss to her lips as she raised herself.

'I have to go,' he said. 'I cannot say for certain how long I will be gone. You only have to ring room service for anything you require. Full English breakfast, if you like,' he added with a smile. 'The staff all speak your language.'

Gina stilled the urge to ask him not to go. Business obviously took precedence this morning. 'What do I do with myself while you're out?' she said instead.

'Whatever you wish,' he rejoined. 'The Colosseum is close by, although I would recommend that you take a taxi if you decide to go there. A woman walking the street alone is apt to attract the kind of attention best not experienced.'

'You mean I might get my bottom pinched?' she said flippantly.

'That could be the least of it.' He didn't look particularly amused. 'Promise me you will take no foolish risks.'

'I won't,' she assured him. 'I'll probably stay around the hotel anyway.'

'It might be best,' he agreed. 'Tonight we will eat at one of Rome's finest restaurants.'

'Can't wait,' Gina murmured, her mind more on the sustenance that would hopefully come later. 'See you later, then.'

She watched him cross the room, appraising the broad-

shouldered, narrow-hipped physique. All man, and all hers:
in bed if not out of it. This marriage might be missing an
ingredient, but what they had was enough to carry it
through—for now, at least. It had to be enough.

Breakfast was brought to the suite by a young and handsome waiter who made it clear that he was open to any
suggestion the 'lovely *signorina*' might have in mind.
More amused than annoyed, Gina despatched him with a
few well-chosen words—a joke she doubted Lucius would
appreciate. Some things were best not shared.

By mid morning she had had enough of being on her
own. She should have plumped for at least a couple of
days in Rome when Lucius had asked where she would
like to spend the honeymoon, she thought ruefully. By the
time he returned it would probably be too late to see anything, and tomorrow they would be motoring south. Providing she stuck to the main thoroughfares, she could
hardly come to much harm.

She put on a pair of beige linen trousers and a short-
sleeved white blouse as the least likely outfit to attract
undue attention. The air outside was hot and humid, the
Via Claudia thronged with traffic. As Lucius had said, the
Colosseum was close enough to walk to.

As he had also said, a woman on her own tended to
draw attention of a less than welcome nature. Gina studi-
ously ignored the whistles and ribald invitations—as she
assumed the latter were from the leers accompanying
them—niftily sidestepping two grinning youths who attempted to bar her way. A bit like running the gauntlet,
she admitted, glad to reach the Colosseum entrance at last.

Despite the crowds, she was overcome by the timeless
spell of the place. Looking down from the terraces on the
crumbling arena, it was all too easy to imagine an age long

gone, when the exposed cells would be filled with wild animals and slaves to be sacrificed for the entertainment of the masses. A cruel age, Gina reflected, thankful not to have lived in those times herself.

She took a taxi from there to St Peter's Square, marvelling along with countless others at the wonders of the Sistine Chapel, then another to see the Trevi Fountain. Hunger finally drew her attention to the time. She was dismayed to see it was already almost three o'clock. Lucius probably wouldn't have returned yet, she assured herself, heading back to the hotel.

She was wrong. Lucius had not only returned, but had been there for the last two hours. He was furious with her. So much so that she was drawn to retaliate with equal ferocity.

'I'm not some chattel to be told what to do and when to do it!' she stormed. 'You left me to twiddle my thumbs with no idea of when you might be back, so you've no room to complain!'

Eyes like black coals, Lucius drew in a harsh breath. 'I will not be spoken to in that manner!' he said in a clipped tone. 'If I have nothing else, I will have your respect!'

About to lash out with further invective, Gina took a hold on herself. Little more than twenty-four hours married and already at loggerheads, she thought dispiritedly. What price the future if this was all it took?

'I apologise,' she said, although it cost her to do it. 'I owe you a great deal, I know.'

'You think I look for gratitude?' he demanded. 'The debt is mine.'

'You think *my* only interest is financial compensation?' she rejoined. 'So far as I'm concerned, the investment you've made in Redman's wipes the slate clean.'

'The investment we both made,' he said. 'Everything I have is now yours too.'

Gina searched the chiselled features in dawning comprehension, mind reeling. 'Was that the business you had to take care of this morning?' she asked faintly.

The dark head inclined. 'My lawyers had the matter already in hand but there was still a great deal to be gone through. As of this day we are partners in every sense.'

Gina sank into the nearest chair, legs suddenly too weak to support her. A fairy tale Isabel had called it, but this went far beyond that.

'There was no need,' she got out. 'I never wanted—'

'It was necessary.' His tone was level, his gaze steady. 'Should anything happen to me, San Cotone will be yours alone, as it would have been had Giovanni lived.'

Alarm leapt in her eyes. 'What do you mean, should anything happen to you? There's nothing wrong with you, is there?'

A smile touched the firm mouth. 'It would pain you to lose me?'

The very thought was a stab in the heart. 'Of course it would!' she said thickly. 'Lucius, what—?'

'So far as I am aware, my health is excellent,' he assured her. 'I spoke only of contingencies. All I ask is that you would care for my family in the event.'

'It goes without saying.' Gina didn't even want to think about such an event. 'I'm sorry about taking off the way I did without even leaving you a note,' she added impulsively. 'It was totally inconsiderate.'

'I will put the blame on your independent English half,' he returned on a lighter note. 'You had no problems?'

She made an effort to match his mood. 'Nothing I couldn't handle. I saw the Colosseum and St Peter's. Oh, and the Trevi Fountain too.'

'You made a wish?'

'No,' she admitted. 'The crowds were too thick to get near enough to toss a coin.'

'Then we must return this evening. Those who visit the Fountain must complete the ritual, or bad luck may befall them. For now, however…' he paused, the smile this time sending her pulse rate soaring '…you wish to continue with your sightseeing?'

Food took second place in the hunger stakes, Gina acknowledged. Would there ever come a time when she failed to want this? she wondered as he took his cue from the shake of her head to draw her into his arms. Right now it seemed impossible.

Capri was as beautiful as Gina had anticipated, although the summer crowds proved something of a drawback. She readily agreed to Lucius's suggestion after a couple of days that they move on, not really caring where they were providing it was together.

The little village in the mainland mountains where they'd spent several precious days and nights was a memory to be treasured. Totally lacking in all but the most basic facilities, though clean as a whistle, the one hotel had boasted just two rooms. Gina had loved every moment of their time there.

Knowing it all had to come to an end eventually made it no easier to accept when the time came. San Cotone might be her home now, but it didn't feel like it. She hated the thought of facing Ottavia's enmity again—and wasn't yet convinced that Cornelia's feelings were any different. Donata was the only one she looked forward to seeing.

They took the train from Naples. Gina grew more despondent with the passing of each mile. She summoned a smile on catching Lucius's eye, reluctant to have him guess her feelings.

'I suppose you already made arrangements for us to be met?'

'Of course,' he confirmed. 'Pietro is to bring a car.'

'Pietro?'

'*Madre's* chauffeur. Tonight we sleep in the suite your grandmother and grandfather would have occupied in their time. The suite your mother and Giovanni would have shared in their turn had he ever completed his journey home.'

'You can't really know what would have happened if he had,' Gina returned. 'His father might not have been prepared to recognise the marriage.'

Lucius gave a brief shrug. 'It would have been up to Giovanni to make him recognise it, but there is little use, I agree, in speculation. It is our place now to extend the Carandente line.'

Towards which end they'd already made serious efforts, Gina reflected, with a familiar stirring in the pit of her stomach at the very thought. She was back to waiting a couple of weeks again before she could be sure, but some inner sense told her it was already an established fact. In nine months she would hold Lucius's child in her arms. Boy or girl didn't matter to her, but it would to him.

The car was already waiting at the station. Pietro greeted the two of them with deference. Gina sat through the journey in growing dread of the ordeal to come. Six short weeks, that was all it had taken to bring her to this point. It hardly seemed possible.

Lit by the evening sun, San Cotone was even more beautiful than she remembered. Stepping from the car, she stood for a moment just gazing at it, unable still to believe it was all hers.

'Welcome home,' said Lucius softly at her back.

Cornelia's appearance in the open doorway cut off any reply Gina might have made. Aided by a walking stick, the older woman limped to the top of the stone steps, her smile a reassurance in itself.

'I have waited so long for this!' she exclaimed. 'Come, *nuora*, let me embrace you!'

Gina went willingly, moved beyond words by the warmth of the greeting. Donata came rushing out to join them, flinging her arms about Gina's neck to hug her with unbridled enthusiasm.

'I'm so happy to have you return to us!' she exclaimed. 'I've had no one to talk with these past weeks!'

Gina made the appropriate responses, wishing she could hope for the same attitude from Ottavia. The latter's absence from the welcome party underlined the unlikelihood.

Donata led the way indoors chattering nineteen to the dozen, Cornelia and Lucius following on. Gina heard her mother-in-law say something in Italian, recognising one word with a sudden dampening of the spirits raised. Livia was the name of the woman Cornelia had proclaimed the ideal wife for her son. Was it possible that the welcome just extended had been no more than a front after all?

Her spirits sank even lower on reaching the salon to see the two people awaiting them. Perhaps a year or so older than herself, Livia Marucchi was one of the most beautiful women she had ever clapped eyes on, her smoothly swathed, blue-black hair drawn back from the perfect oval of her face. There was no warmth in the smile that touched her lips as she looked from Gina to the man at her back.

'I offer my congratulations,' she said in heavily accented English.

There was no telling anything from Lucius's voice when he thanked her. Gina refrained from glancing his way as he moved to her side to perform the unnecessary introduction, summoning a smile of her own. 'Nice to meet you,' she lied.

The curl of Livia's lip was slight enough to go unnoted by most. 'And you also,' she said.

Silent so far, Ottavia came forward to take Gina by the shoulders and place a kiss to both cheeks, the glitter in her eyes the only indication of her true feelings. 'So we are sisters now!'

If Lucius had any inkling of his sister's frame of mind he wasn't allowing it to affect him. 'You will excuse us if we leave you so soon,' he said evenly. 'We are both in need of a shower and change of clothing after our journey.'

Gina accompanied him from the room feeling anything but happy. She longed to be back in the village they had left that morning.

'I didn't ask if the things I had sent from home had arrived,' she said as they mounted the stairs.

'This is your home now,' Lucius responded a little curtly. 'You must begin thinking of it as such.'

She gave him a swift glance, noting the set of his jaw. There was a difference in him since their arrival: a change of mood attributable to Livia Marucchi, if she was any judge at all. Donata had given the impression that her brother had had no intention of marrying the woman, but what would she have really known of his plans?

The suite they were to occupy was on the far side of the villa from the room that had been hers before. Her mind on other matters, Gina viewed the spacious, beautifully furnished rooms with scant interest. Her things had indeed arrived, she saw on opening one of the vast wardrobes in the dressing area. It was going to take a great deal more clothing than she possessed in total to fill even one of them.

There were two bathrooms, each superbly equipped. Lucius was already in the shower, the closed door a barrier she wouldn't have thought twice about breaching only yesterday. It was ridiculous feeling this way on the strength of one short meeting, she told herself hardily. If Lucius had wanted to marry Livia he would have done it before she ever came on the scene. She had to put the whole thing from mind.

He was fully dressed when she emerged from the other bathroom some fifteen minutes later.

'Useful when time presses, perhaps,' he said drily when she commented on the advantages of the arrangement. 'Did you not wish to join me?'

'I wasn't sure you'd want me to,' Gina admitted, drawing a line between the dark brows.

'You consider the home no place for such behaviour?'

'Of course not.' She tried to make light of the situation. 'I suppose I just feel a bit inhibited with all the family here.'

'It is most unlikely that any of them would intrude on our privacy.'

'I'm sure. It's not—' She broke off, spreading her hands with a wry little smile. 'Getting used to being here on a permanent basis at all is going to take time. It was never part of the plan.' She hesitated before putting the question. 'Do they know…everything?'

The shrug was brief. 'I keep no secrets.'

'How did they take it?'

'My mother is already well-provided for, and Donata will no doubt marry well in time.'

His tone discouraged further enquiry, but Gina refused to leave it there. 'And Ottavia?'

'She and Marcello would be reliant on your charity for a time should the need arise.'

'Is that fair?' Gina protested. 'Surely provision can be made!'

'That decision is no longer mine alone,' Lucius returned. 'As I told you, everything I have is now yours too. If I die before you, it will all be yours.'

A sudden little shudder ran through her. To never see him again, never feel his arms about her again...

'If I have a say in things, then I'd like Ottavia and Marcello to be provided for now,' she declared. 'Enough for them to make a new life for themselves without having to rely on family charity.'

'You think Marcello so lacking in pride that he would accept such a gift?' Lucius asked on a note of anger. 'You believe *me* so devoid in humanity that I offered him no other choice than to become comptroller? He chose to draw a salary. One sufficient—if properly invested—to enable him to achieve independence again in the not-too-distant future by his own efforts.'

Gina bit her lip. 'I'm sorry. I should have known better.'

'We have a great deal to learn about each other.' The anger had gone from his voice, replaced by a flatness of tone that was even less desirable. 'It will, as you said, take time.'

Uncertain of his response, Gina quelled the impulse to reach out to him as he turned away. He was right, of course, she thought depressedly. Outside of bed, they were still almost total strangers.

CHAPTER EIGHT

It was a relief not to see Livia when they went down to join the family on the terrace at nine. Gina wouldn't have put it past Ottavia to insist that the woman stayed to dinner. Knowing what she knew, she could understand something of her sister-in-law's feelings. To be ousted from inheritance by someone she hadn't even known existed a couple of months ago took some getting over. It was improbable that they could ever become friends.

If Donata felt done down in any way herself, she gave no sign of it. Her hair had grown considerably in the last month, although it was going to take a year or more for it to achieve any real length.

'I've grown used to it,' she acknowledged cheerfully when Gina commented on the difference. 'I may even keep it short. It's so much cooler in summer!'

'You will never find a husband looking the way you do,' declared Ottavia. 'A woman's hair is her crowning glory! Providing, of course, that she puts both the time and the effort into keeping it so.'

A dig at her, Gina gathered, catching the sly, sideways glance. One she could ignore in the knowledge that her own hair was in no way neglected. For a moment she found herself wishing she was blonde like her mother, just to be different, but the feeling soon passed. She was a Carandente in looks as well as name.

'With a face and figure like Donata's, I'd doubt any man is going to bemoan the lack of a little hair length,' she said with purpose. 'Where I come from, she'd cause riots in the streets!'

'When can I go?' asked Donata promptly, eyes sparkling.

'I think it can be safely said that you caused enough mayhem already in your life,' commented her brother with a sternness belied by the twitching of his lips. 'I shall have a great deal of sympathy for the man who is foolish enough to make you his wife. He will never know a moment's peace of mind again.'

'Cesare has sadly neglected us these past weeks,' observed Ottavia with a malice Gina could have hit her for. 'Perhaps he found himself more pressing interests.'

The sparkle died from Donata's eyes, though she kept her head high. 'I no longer have feelings for Cesare,' she declared, 'so your spitefulness goes unrewarded.'

So put that in your pipe and smoke it! thought Gina, delighted with if not entirely convinced by the response. Ottavia's sisterly empathies left a whole lot to be desired. She looked distinctly put out by her failure to gain a rise.

She answered in rapid Italian, the tone alone enough to convey the meaning of the words spilling from her lips. Lucius put a stop to it with a tersely spoken sentence in the same language. Master of the household in every sense, Gina reflected as Ottavia lapsed into silence.

She felt sympathy for Marcello who was obviously discomfited by the episode. Hopefully for him, it wouldn't be too long before he gained that independence. Not that having Ottavia for a wife could be any picnic. It was surprising that she'd stuck by him at all.

Of them all, Cornelia seemed the least affected by the altercation. Gina doubted if anything ever really upset her. With Lucius married, and likely to produce a grandson to secure the future, she could live out her life however it suited her. In many ways she could be envied.

Tired from the journey, Gina found herself nodding off over coffee, but hesitated to take her departure before Lucius was ready to retire for the night. By the time he did make a move she was almost dead on her feet.

For the very first time she was unable to summon a response when he turned to her in bed, try as she might to keep her mind focused.

'I'm just so tired,' she murmured apologetically. 'If I could just have an hour or two's sleep.'

'There is no compulsion,' Lucius answered drily. 'We have a lifetime ahead. The rest will benefit us both.'

Weary as she was, Gina couldn't deny the pang as he settled himself for sleep. The least he could do was put an arm about her—make her feel wanted for more than just conscience and sex alone. Was he thinking about Livia Marucchi? she wondered dully. Did he wish it was she who shared his bed?

It was just coming light when she awoke. Less than three-and-a-half hours' sleep, she calculated, stretching a cautious arm to turn the bedside clock, yet she felt fully revitalised.

Lying on his back, Lucius was still in the land of nod, his breathing deep and even. He had thrown back the covering sheet in the night, revealing the full length of his body. In the past week, Gina had grown accustomed to sleeping in the nude herself, delighting in the freedom from restraint. Looking at him now, outlined against the pale grey of the window, she felt the familiar stirring in the centre of her body, the quickening of her pulses.

It took everything she had to stop herself from reaching out to waken him with a caress usually guaranteed to create instant arousal. She had refused him last night; why should she expect him to respond to her this morning?

She turned away from him, gazing sightlessly at the far wall. One thing she had learned these last weeks was that real love didn't have to come as a blinding flash, but could grow from a far greater depth through knowledge of a person. Lucius was a man infinitely worthy of love, a man any woman would find it difficult not to love. She might rebel at times against his masculine dominance, yet that in itself was an intrinsic part of his attraction.

What she didn't, and might never have, was his love in return. Not the kind she wanted from him anyway.

Getting through those first days of residence at the villa proved far from easy. There were times when Gina would have given almost anything to turn back the clock. She'd been happy enough in ignorance of all this. Sooner or later she would have met a man she could feel enough for to marry and have children by. A man whose lovemaking would have laboured under no comparison because there would have been none to make.

Where the latter was concerned, she certainly had no cause for complaint. Lucius kept her fully indulged. It was so simple for a man, she often reflected in the darkness when she lay listening to his even breathing and envying him the ability to sleep: the deeper emotions held so much less significance. She was the one who longed to hear the words themselves. Only it wasn't the way he felt about her, and he was no hypocrite.

Suspicion hardened into certainty as the days passed. The thought of the life growing inside her gave rise to a whole new set of emotions. The first of at least three, she decided, having yearned all her life for a brother or sister.

For Lucius's sake, she hoped this one was a boy; so far as she was concerned, good health would be enough.

It was only through Donata that she discovered Lucius had a birthday coming up. Ottavia, she was sure, would have allowed her to continue in ignorance until the day itself, while Cornelia would have probably taken it for granted that she already knew. She resolved to save the news of her pregnancy until then as an extra special present to be given in private, in the meantime racking her brain for some idea on the public front.

In the end she settled on a modernistic Tuscany landscape by an artist she had heard Lucius mention in approving terms, signing the considerable cheque with a sense of burning the final bridge behind her. She not only bore the Carandente blood and name, but was now a fully fledged member of the money-no-object brigade.

Lucius received the painting with gratifying expressions of pleasure. It would, he declared, take pride of place in the study. Gina hugged the knowledge of the present still to come to herself as she watched him open gifts from the rest of the family. Cornelia had arranged a luncheon party in celebration of the event, though not with her son's approval. He would, Gina gathered, prefer to spend the day like any other.

'I grew out of birthday parties long ago,' he said when she commented on his lack of enthusiasm. '*Madre*, unfortunately, refuses to accept it. If this occasion follows the pattern of previous years, there will be champagne in which to toast my continuing health and prosperity.'

'I'll drink to that,' Gina rejoined. 'The health part anyway.'

Lucius raised a quizzical eyebrow. 'You have no interest in prosperity?'

'Money isn't everything.'

'You told me that once before,' he said. 'But you have to admit that it has its uses. Without it, San Cotone would not exist.'

They were in the study, where he had insisted on coming to hang the painting himself. Looking at him as he leaned against the desk edge to admire the landscape, Gina was reminded of the very first time she had set eyes on him. The attraction that had flared in her that day bore no comparison with what she felt for him now.

'I have something to tell you,' she said softly, unable to wait any longer. 'You're going to be a father.'

He came slowly upright from the desk, the dark eyes meeting hers holding an expression that lifted her spirits even further.

'You are certain?' he asked.

'As much as I can be without confirmation from other sources.'

Lucius came over to where she stood, taking her in his arms to deliver a heart-stirring kiss. '*Madre* will be delighted.'

'Providing it's a boy.'

Dark brows lifted quizzically. 'You believe she would look on a girl with disfavour?'

'I believe she might regard *me* with disfavour for producing one.'

Lucius smiled and shook his head. 'The gender is decided by the particular sperm that first reaches the egg, so if anyone is to be held responsible it would be the father. She will, I assure you, receive whatever we produce with open arms.'

Blue eyes bored into his, doing their utmost to penetrate the impenetrable. 'You don't care about carrying on the Carandente name?'

'Naturally I care. The three hundred years of our ancestry makes it imperative that I make every effort to extend it. But if I fail…' he lifted his shoulders '…then, I fail. The world will carry on without us.'

'We don't have to stop at the one in any case,' said Gina impulsively. 'Children need companionship.'

Lucius reached out a hand to smooth the hair back from her face in a gesture so tender it moved her immeasurably. 'You felt the lack of siblings yourself?'

'Yes,' she admitted.

'Your parents had no desire for a family?'

'I think it was more a case of it simply not happening for them.' Gina lightened her voice, bearing down on the urge to declare her love for him there and then. 'The Carandente virility isn't given to every man.'

'I knew failure myself not long ago,' Lucius reminded her. 'Your stepfather is no exception.'

He drew her to him, his kiss this time stimulating a passionate response. Gina knew real regret when he released her again, wishing now that she had waited to tell him about the baby until later when they were unlikely to be interrupted by anyone.

If Lucius suffered the same degree of frustration, his smile as he touched her lips with a fingertip was steady enough.

'With all respect to your instincts, I think it best that we keep the news to ourselves until we have the confirmation you spoke of. I'll make an arrangement for you to see a physician.'

It made sense, Gina supposed. 'That's the first contraction I ever heard you use,' she remarked brightly.

He laughed. 'My English improves by leaps and bounds, as you would say! Soon I'll be speaking it like a native!'

'Not with that accent,' she teased. 'You sound like an

Italian film star all the girls in school used to be crazy about.'

Amusement curved the strong mouth. 'Including yourself?'

'Oh, definitely! He was a real hunk! A bit old, I suppose, thinking about it. He must have been all of thirty-four or five.'

The amusement deepened. 'Tonight,' he promised, 'I will show you what an old man of thirty-four is capable of!'

Gina pulled a face at him, wishing it was tonight already. 'I tremble at the thought!'

'Our guests will soon begin arriving,' declared Cornelia from the open doorway. 'Do you not think it time to prepare for their reception?'

'Of course,' Gina said hurriedly. 'I hadn't realised it was that late.' She hesitated, mindful of the decision already made, yet yearning to tell her mother-in-law the news she knew for certain to be a fact not a fancy. 'Is it to be a very dressy affair?' was all she could think of to say instead.

'No more than you care to make it,' said Lucius. 'Go on ahead. I'll follow in a moment or two.'

Gina would rather he accompanied her now, but with Cornelia there, hardly felt able to make the request. She left the two of them, and headed upstairs, still not at all sure what she should wear for this luncheon party. The buffet was to be served on the terrace, which suggested a certain informality. The white linen tunic she had bought last week and not yet worn should be suitable.

She was already changed when Lucius came up. He closeted himself immediately in his bathroom. As he had made no comment on her choice of dress, Gina could only assume it was suitable to the occasion. Considering the price of it, it darn well should be, she thought, viewing her slender curves in the cheval mirror.

With her legs tanned golden brown, she had deemed the wearing of stockings unnecessary. The kitten-heeled sandals were designed for comfort as well as style; if she was going to be on her feet for two or three hours, the former was essential. Her only jewellery was the single strand of cultured pearls given her by her parents on her eighteenth birthday, along with the filigree silver watch Lucius had bought her in Rome.

Plus her engagement ring, of course. She held up her hand so that the stone caught the light from the window, wishing now that she hadn't allowed Lucius to talk her out of the simple hoop she would have chosen for herself. The solitaire could hardly be called ostentatious, she had to admit, but it was still too much of a statement of worth for her tastes.

She was still standing there watching the colours dance when Lucius emerged from the bathroom. He was nude but for the black silk boxer shorts he had taken in with him, his skin gleaming with health and vitality.

'I thought you would have gone down by now,' he commented.

'It's your birthday not mine,' Gina returned lightly. 'You're the one people will want to see.'

'On the contrary, *you* will be the main attraction. Some will be attending only in order to meet the woman of my choice.'

Except that he'd had no choice, Gina reflected. Not in his estimation, at any rate.

'We call it vetting in my country,' she said, trying for a jocular note.

Pulling on a cream silk shirt, Lucius gave her a slightly sharpened glance. '*This* is your country now.'

'It's where I live,' she responded. 'I still hold a British passport.'

'Born of an Italian father, you will have little difficulty obtaining full citizenship.'

'Always providing I want to become an Italian citizen.'

Lucius stopped buttoning buttons to gaze at her in some exasperation. 'With an Italian father and husband, why would you wish otherwise?'

Up until that moment, Gina had to confess, she had given the matter little if any consideration. Now, she found herself struggling for words to convey what she felt.

'My mother is English. I was brought up to English ways. I can't turn my back on twenty-five years of my life.'

'You think I would ask it of you?'

'Isn't that just what you are doing?' she said. 'I don't *feel* Italian. Not in any sense. Why should it be taken for granted that I'll be prepared to become one?'

'If for no other reason, to honour your father's memory. Had he lived, you would have known no other life.'

'There's no certainty of that even if he had lived.'

Lucius shook his head emphatically. 'With a child on the way the marriage would have been accepted.' He held up a staying hand as she opened her mouth to dispute the statement. 'You have no basis for disagreement. I knew my cousin. You did not.'

Gina had to give best on that score. What she couldn't do was let the rest pass. 'I'm staying British,' she stated flatly.

The dark eyes acquired a sudden steely core. 'You must do as you wish, of course, but our children will take their father's nationality as is customary.'

He turned away to finish his dressing. Gina looked on silently as he donned one of the pale-shaded suits that sat his lithe frame so well, wishing now that she'd tackled the subject in a less confrontational manner. Not that she'd any intention of changing her mind. Her own feelings apart, it would be like a kick in the face for her mother.

When it came to their children, she didn't have much of a leg to stand on. They would learn to speak English as a matter of course, but it would be Italy they regarded as their homeland. She had to accept that.

'It seems like it might be a dressier occasion than I thought,' she commented as Lucius finished fastening gold cuff-links. 'Should I choose something else?'

He ran a cursory glance over her, expression unrevealing. 'I see no reason for it. Your taste, as always, is impeccable. We must go.'

People were already beginning to arrive when they got downstairs. Over the course of the next half hour, Gina was kissed on both cheeks so many times she lost count. Speculation was rife among both male and female alike. She wondered just how much was known of her background.

Thankful to see someone she already knew, she greeted Cesare with pleasure.

'Why have you left it this long to come over?' she asked, drawing him aside. 'We've been back almost two weeks!'

'I was out of the country myself until yesterday,' he acknowledged. 'I was given the news only last night.'

'It must have been quite a shock for you,' Gina said softly.

His smile was a reassurance in itself. 'Lucius had already acquainted me with the fact of your birthright—and with his intention to right the wrong done to you. Giovanni can now rest easy in his grave.' He studied her for a moment. 'You are happy, yes?'

'Of course,' she said. 'Who wouldn't be happy to have all this?'

Cesare looked a little uncertain. 'But you have some regard for Lucius too, I trust?'

'Of course,' she said again, wishing she could tell him—tell anyone—just how much. 'I couldn't have married a man I didn't have any feeling for at all. And what about you?' she went on, eager to change the subject. 'Did you find the girl of your dreams yet?'

The wicked sparkle she remembered leapt in his eyes. 'The girl of my dreams has been taken from me by another, so I must look afresh.'

'You could do worse than Donata,' Gina murmured.

'I could indeed,' he agreed surprisingly. 'I thought about her much these past weeks.' He cast a glance around. 'She is here today?'

'Somewhere, yes.' Gina tried not to let her hopes for her younger sister-in-law rise too high. 'Look for a scarlet dress. Not that she's likely to stand out at a glance,' she added on a humorous note. 'I seem to be the only bird around with dull plumage!'

Cesare made a slow and lingering scrutiny of her arresting face with its wide-spaced, vivid eyes and full-lipped rosy mouth, the glossy cascade of black hair. 'Your plumage,' he declared, 'could never be anything but dazzling! Lucius is a fortunate man.'

But did he know it? she thought, spirits taking an abrupt dive as her gaze went beyond Cesare to the couple seemingly engrossed in conversation a short distance away. Livia Marucchi looked divine in a form-fitting dress the colour of ripe apricots, her feet clad in a mere whisper of light tan leather. From the way Lucius was looking into the eyes fixed on his, no one else existed.

She should have known, of course, that the woman

would be invited. As a long-standing friend of Ottavia's—
to say nothing of Lucius himself—she would hardly have
been left out. The question uppermost in her mind right
now was just how close that latter relationship had been.

'Was there anything between Lucius and Livia before I
came on the scene?' she heard herself asking.

Cesare looked disconcerted. 'That is a question only
Lucius can answer.'

'I know.' Gina already regretted the unstudied enquiry.
'I'm sorry, Cesare. I shouldn't have asked.'

'Livia is not a woman I would have chosen to relate
with myself, if that is of any help,' he proffered after a
moment.

Meaning what? she itched to know. It was unlikely that
she left him physically unstirred: it would be against nature
for any hot-blooded Italian male to look at a woman of
Livia Marucchi's undoubted beauty and feel no effect in
his loins. It was obvious however that he'd said all he was
going to say on the subject.

When she looked again, both Lucius and Livia had disappeared. To where, and for what, she didn't care to consider.

Donata came weaving through the throng, the scarlet
dress emphasising every line of her supple young body.
The flower in her hair was scarlet too, perfectly matched
by the colour of her lips. Flamboyant, perhaps, Gina
thought fondly, but it suited her.

She greeted Cesare in Italian, her manner easy. He responded in the same vein. An act on both parts, Gina
judged, watching the two of them as they chatted. Her
Italian was still too limited to understand more than a few
words, especially at the pace in which they were speaking,
but the nuances came through loud and clear.

It was Donata who called a halt, apologising in English for her discourtesy.

'I'm hardly going to improve my grasp if everyone speaks English all the time for my benefit,' Gina reassured her. 'I hope to be bilingual by this time next year.'

This time next year she would be a mother too, came the thought. Whether she would be any closer to knowing the man she had married was something else.

She had been aware for some time of a man on the periphery of her vision who appeared to be watching her. Murmuring something about circulating, she moved on, donning a social smile as the man stepped smoothly into her path. She couldn't recall having seen him prior to this moment.

'Mario Lanciani,' he supplied. 'I have waited so long to speak with you alone.'

'About what?' Gina asked.

The good-looking if somewhat dissipated features creased in a smile. 'To speak is perhaps the wrong word. I wish only to tell you that your beauty outshines that of every other woman here today!'

As a line, Gina reflected, she'd heard better. She kept a straight face with an effort. 'You're very flattering, Signor Lanciani.'

'Mario,' he said. 'You must call me Mario if we are going to be friends.'

The straight face was even harder to maintain this time. '*Are* we going to be friends?'

'But of course,' he said. 'You feel what I feel myself. I see it in your eyes.'

It was reprehensible to play him along, but Gina found the temptation too much to resist. He was so utterly confident of his charms. She infused a note of regret in her voice. 'Some things we must fight against.'

Outside of lovemaking, she had never seen a man smoulder before, but she was seeing it now, feigned though she took the emotion to be. 'Why must we?' he demanded softly.

Enough was enough, Gina told herself: in fact, more than enough in this case. 'I have a husband,' she said, letting him down more gently than he merited.

The shrug was dismissive. 'He has liaisons outside of the marital bed, so why should you not?'

She should treat the suggestion with contempt, Gina knew, but her better judgement had gone for a walk. 'With whom?' She jerked the words out.

'Why, Livia Marucchi, of course.' He made it sound as if she shouldn't have needed to ask. 'It is no secret. Doubt-less there are others too. Lucius is the kind of man for whom one woman could never be enough.'

Gina bit back the instinctive retort. It was no more than she had thought herself on more than one occasion. 'I think you'd better leave,' she managed with a fair degree of control.

'A pity.' He sighed. 'I believed you a woman of the world.'

She turned on her heel and left him there, not trusting her tongue to stay cleaved to the roof of her mouth for much longer. They had been under surveillance by people in the vicinity, she realised, catching a glance or two in passing. She donned a smile. However bad she might feel inside, she was dammed if anyone else was going to know about it.

CHAPTER NINE

As Lucius had predicted, Cornelia called for a toast to be drunk. What Gina had not anticipated was her own inclusion in the pledge, although she should have realised that the party served a dual purpose in celebrating both birthday and marriage. She set herself to show no resistance when Lucius drew her to him to kiss her first on each cheek, and then on the lips, to smile into his eyes despite her conviction that hers wasn't the only mouth he'd kissed in the last hour.

'Long life and happiness,' she echoed in English, careful to iron out any hint of sarcasm from her tone.

Not quite careful enough though, if the sudden narrowing of the dark eyes was anything to go by. Lucius was all too capable of seeing through the dissimulation.

He kept her by his side for the following half hour or so, an arm about her waist, his hand resting lightly on her hip-bone. There was no sign of Livia. Not that it made any difference, Gina admitted. The woman was here in spirit if not in actual presence.

It was almost five o'clock before the last guest drifted away. With several hours to fill until dinner, and reluctant to spend them alone with Lucius, Gina took herself off into the gardens. The weather had turned sultry, with a heavy build-up of cloud gradually blotting out the blue. They were probably in for a storm, the first she'd have known in this neck of the woods.

Despite the lower heels, her sandals weren't all that

comfortable when it came to extended walking. She took them off in the end and continued in bare feet, sticking to the grass as much as possible and enjoying the feel of it between her toes. She still found it difficult to realise that all this splendour was her home. She doubted she would ever learn to take it for granted, the way her children would in time to come.

Children? Right now, she could conjure little enthusiasm for the one already on the way. There was still a possibility that she was wrong anyway.

Unlikely, she was bound to admit. She'd always been regular as clockwork. In nine months, minus a week or two, she would be giving birth to a son or daughter who would never go short of anything money could provide.

She had wandered out of the formal gardens and into one of the old olive groves edging them, she realised, coming down to earth again. The sudden, startling lightning flash was followed by a clap of thunder right overhead, deafening her for a moment or two as it rolled around the heavens.

Gina sought shelter under a tree as the rain came pelting down with the force of a sledgehammer, but the protection was minimal. There was a tumbledown hut some short distance away. Too wet already to care over-much, she made her way across to it, sinking to a seat on the rough bench running around three sides to view the unremitting downpour through the doorless doorway with unthrilled eyes. It was obviously going to be some time before she could make her way back to the villa, and no one would know where she was. The thought that Lucius might be concerned was somewhat satisfying.

She could hardly believe it when the next flash of lightning revealed the figure dashing through the trees towards the hut. The thunder this time was a little further away, but still loud enough to drown out the words spilling from Lucius's lips as he gained shelter. He was furious, that much she could tell, furious and soaked, his suit a sodden ruin.

'How did you find me?' was all she could think of to say for the moment.

'You were seen heading in this direction,' he snapped. 'What possessed you to come so far with a storm about to break?'

'I didn't notice the cloud coming up until the sun disappeared,' she prevaricated. 'Anyway, you didn't need to come looking for me. I'm a big girl. Storms don't scare me.'

The anger suffusing his face in no way diminished. '*I* will scare you if you ever do this to me again!' he threatened. 'You could have been struck by the lightning and killed—along with the child you are carrying!'

'Which would concern you most?' The question was out before she could stop it, wiping his face clear of all expression as he gazed at her.

'You think me capable of such a choice?' he said at length.

Gina would have given a great deal to turn back the clock just a few minutes. She would rather face his anger, she reflected wryly, than this total blanking out of emotion.

'No,' she said. 'Of course not. I was being...' She broke off, spreading her hands in a helpless little gesture. 'I'm not sure what I was being. Can we forget it?'

'You must have had reason to ask such a question,' Lucius persisted. 'Why should such a thought even cross your mind?'

'I *wasn't* thinking. It was a stupid thing to say at all.'

He studied her a moment longer, then abruptly inclined his head. 'Very well, it's forgotten.'

It wasn't, and wouldn't be, she was certain, but at least she was off the hook for now. She sought a safer topic. 'Is it going to be a long storm, do you think?'

'Long enough for alarm to be raised when we fail to make our appearance,' he said.

'You mean *you* neglected to tell anyone where you were going too?'

The sarcasm lit fresh sparks in the dark eyes. 'My tolerance is stretched very fine,' he warned.

'It must be my hormones,' she claimed, seeking refuge in humour. 'Indulge me, will you?'

His smile was brief. 'It appears I must.'

He slid off his jacket, hanging it on a jutting edge of the rough stone wall. The rain had penetrated through to the shirt beneath in huge damp patches. He took that off too.

'You should remove your outer clothing,' he advised, viewing her saturated dress. 'Better by far than sitting in it until the rain ceases.' He was unzipping his trousers as he spoke, sliding the clinging material down his legs and kicking off his shoes in order to remove the garment and hang it to join the other items. 'We're fortunate here in retaining the warmth when it storms.'

Gina put her tongue to lips gone suddenly dry as she contemplated the superb physique. The black silk shorts he favoured did little to conceal the swell of his manhood. Despite all Mario had said, she wanted him so badly it was like a fire lit inside her, spreading rapidly into every part of her.

He knew it too. It was there in his eyes as he looked at her—in the slow, sensual widening of his lips. He came over to where she sat and drew her unprotestingly to her feet, turning her about to slide the long back-zip of her dress and ease it from her shoulders. Despite the heat, she shivered to his touch, limbs quivering, insides turning to molten lava as he unclipped the flimsy lace bra and slid both hands beneath to cup the firm curves.

'*Bella!*' he murmured.

The dress fell unheeded to the dry earth floor. Gina leaned against him, eyes closed, relishing the feel of the warm bare flesh at her back, the possessiveness in his touch. It didn't have to be true, she told herself. None of it was true!

He lowered his head to kiss the side of her neck, his lips leaving a trail of fire as they moved slowly upwards. The sensation when he ran the tip of his tongue over the rim of her ear to nuzzle the sensitive lobe was indescribable. Shuddering, she twisted in his arms to press her lips into the coating of hair on his chest, tasting the faint, salty tang of a dampness that had nothing to do with the rain.

The silk shorts were no obstacle. Gina followed them down the muscular length of his legs to remove them completely. It was Lucius's turn to shudder, his whole body tensing to the exquisite embrace. He stood it for no more than a few seconds before drawing her upright again to kiss her with a passion that fired her to even greater heights, murmuring guttural, indistinguishable words against her lips.

There was no softness in the earth floor, but she was past caring about such creature comforts. She lifted her head to look down the length of her body as he poised himself above her, thrilling to the size of him, the leashed power. He entered her slowly, purposefully, watching her face contort as he began the movement she craved. Gina wrapped her legs about the hard, masculine hips as the world came crashing in on them.

It took the sight of her dirt-streaked arms cradling the dark head against her breast to bring her back to reality again. The floor had been dry, her skin and hair hadn't; she must, she thought, look as if she'd taken a mud bath!

'I'm a mess!' she exclaimed. 'How on earth am I going to get cleaned up?'

Lucius lifted himself up to survey her, lips twitching. 'A little less impeccable than before, I agree.'

'Not just me!' she pointed out, eyes seeking the white dress crumpled where it had fallen. 'How can I put that back on?'

'One problem at a time.' He pressed himself to his feet, reaching a hand to pull her to hers. 'The rain is still heavy enough.'

They were outside in it before Gina could find breath to protest. Not that she could come up with a better idea, she acknowledged as the water sluiced over her. She gave in to it, laughing as she raked her hands through her hair to cleanse it of the clinging earth, the streaks running down her body.

Lucius had picked up comparatively little himself. Standing there, body glistening, he exemplified physical perfection: a Michelangelo masterpiece come to vibrant life. She wanted him again, right there and then. Sheer gluttony, she admonished herself.

His damp shirt was little help in drying themselves, although they did the best they could. Gina grimaced as she donned the scraps of underwear and pulled on the badly soiled and crumpled dress.

'I don't suppose there's a secret passage we can get back indoors by?'

Lucius laughed and shook his head. 'Unfortunately no.'

'It's all right for you,' she complained. 'You took care to keep *your* things out of the dirt. What's going to be thought when I turn up like this!'

'That you had a fall,' he said without undue concern.

'It would be probable enough in such a torrent. It will cease shortly now that the storm centre has passed over us. We may even see blue skies again before nightfall.'

The rain was certainly lessening. Gina glanced at her watch, surprised in the circumstances to find it still going—even more surprised to find that barely an hour had passed since her departure from the villa.

'Are they likely to send search parties out for us?' she asked.

'After several more hours perhaps. As we are already so wet, there seems little point in lingering further. You should put on your shoes,' he added. 'They will afford some protection for your feet.'

The state they were in, Gina doubted it, but she complied anyway. Worms liked the wet, and she hated the thought of stepping on one.

Even with the rain letting up, it was hard going through the long grass. Gina was relieved to reach the narrow path she had been following when the storm had begun. Lucius supported her with a hand under her elbow until they were back in the cultivated grounds where the way was smoother.

They entered the villa by a side door. Thinking they'd got away with it when they reached the main staircase without running into anyone, Gina froze with her foot on the first step as the *salotto* door opened.

It had to be Ottavia, of course. And she wasn't alone. Livia looked equally dumbfounded on sight of them.

'We were caught in the storm,' said Lucius before either woman could speak. 'You will excuse us if we go straight away to find dry clothing.'

He urged Gina on up the stairs with a hand in the small of her back, a direction she wasn't loath to take. If it had been Ottavia on her own it wouldn't have mattered as much, but to appear in this state before the woman she still believed was something more to Lucius than a mere friend of the family—even if not to the extent Mario had intimated—was unbearably humiliating.

They reached their suite without a further word passing between them. Lucius strode directly across to his bathroom, leaving Gina to strip off the ruined dress and step under her own shower.

She washed her hair first, rinsing it thoroughly before soaping her body. The euphoria she had felt back there in the hut had vanished completely. She'd given him nothing he wouldn't have experienced before, and no doubt with a great deal more expertise. She was a pure beginner when it came to sexual stimulation, while he knew every move in the book. If not already seeking other outlets, how long would it be before he became bored enough to do it?

Wearing a bathrobe much like her own, he was lounging on the bed when she finally emerged.

'I was beginning to think you had fallen asleep,' he remarked. 'What could have taken so long when the dirt was all but removed already?'

'I felt like a good long soak, that's all,' she said.

'Then, you should have run a bath.' He allowed his gaze to drift the length of her body and back again, his slow smile starting the all too familiar strumming on her heart strings. 'Come here to me,' he invited softly.

Something in her refused to give way to the urge. 'I need to dry my hair,' she said. 'It takes hours!'

'Something of an exaggeration, I think.' His tone was dry. 'Perhaps I can help speed the process.'

He got up from the bed and walked over to the dressing table to take her dryer from its drawer. Plugging it into the nearby socket, he switched it on and picked up a brush, turning to look at her with lifted brows.

'The sooner we begin, the sooner we finish.'

Short of telling him to get lost, Gina was left with little choice but to let him have his way. She took a seat on the padded stool, watching through the mirror as he lifted the first thick strands and got to work.

It felt good, she had to admit. He showed a rare dexterity in his use of both brush and dryer.

'It isn't the first time you've done this, is it?' she felt moved to ask.

'The first time in practice,' he acknowledged. 'I used to watch my mother dry her hair when I was a boy. It always fascinated me to see the difference emerge.'

'You might have been a hairdresser in a previous life,' she said lightly. 'Did you ever try regressing?'

'A waste of both time and energy,' he returned. 'We have the one life to make the best of.'

The one life into which to pack as much as possible was what he meant, Gina surmised, unable to keep the doubts at bay any longer. Why should a wife curtail that aim?

'Might you have married Livia Marucchi?' she heard herself asking without conscious intention, and saw the face in the mirror acquire an indecipherable expression.

'At no time,' he said.

'Why not?' she insisted. 'She's surely everything any man could want?'

'In the purely physical sense, perhaps. I had other requirements in a wife.'

Gina swallowed on the hard lump in her throat. There was no point in feeling hurt by the admission that he found the woman physically desirable when she'd already suggested as much.

'You mean she wasn't a virgin,' she said flatly. 'Didn't she know how you felt about that?'

'I never discussed it with her.'

'But you have slept with her?'

The reply was a moment or two coming, his expression still giving little away. 'Nothing that happened before you came into my life has any relevance,' he said at length. 'It's the future that matters not the past.'

Gina said softly, 'You see us growing old together?'

'The fates providing. Marriage, in my mind, is for life.'

How about marital fidelity? she yearned to ask, but doubted that she would get an honest reply.

'Mine too,' she returned, and saw a smile widen the firm mouth.

'It had better be.'

Her hair was dry enough by now to be brushed into order. Lucius switched off the dryer and unplugged it, rolling the flex around the handle before putting it back in the drawer he'd taken it from.

'We have an hour to spare before we need dress for dinner,' he observed, watching her smooth the shining tresses.

'So read a book,' she suggested, stifling her involuntary response. 'Improve your mind.'

The smile came again. 'You think my mind in need of improvement?'

'I think it's possible to have too much of a good thing,' she said with purpose, needing to get at him in some way. '"Surfeiting, the appetite may sicken, and so die."'

His shrug made light of the intimation. 'Your Shakespeare was a man of many words.'

Regret came swift and sharp as he turned away. If she wanted him to go looking elsewhere for sex, she was going the right way about it. It was hardly as if she found his appetite for lovemaking any hardship. She was usually of the same mind.

*   *   *

Livia, it turned out, was not only staying on to dinner, but had been invited to spend the night—by whom, it wasn't clear. Gina found herself analysing every word and glance that passed between Lucius and the other woman. Ridiculous, she knew, but she couldn't help herself.

It was Ottavia who brought the conversation round to the luncheon party.

'I saw you talking with Mario Lanciani,' she said to Gina. 'You should be cautious in your dealings with a man of his kind.'

'What kind is that?' Gina asked.

'Why was he here at all?' Lucius demanded of his mother before his sister could answer.

Cornelia shook her head in obvious bafflement. 'He was not invited.'

Lucius turned his attention to Gina, his expression no encouragement. 'What was it you spoke of with him?'

'We just passed the time of day,' she claimed, not about to admit the truth.

Livia gave a laugh. 'Then, he is indeed changed!'

'You know him so well?' Gina challenged.

'His reputation is known to everyone,' came the smooth reply. 'Many women find him captivating.'

Looking at her, Gina wondered if anyone else saw the malice glistening in her eyes. She had a sudden notion that Mario Lanciani's gatecrashing this afternoon had been orchestrated for him; he certainly hadn't put up much of a struggle to retain her company once the message had been delivered, and she'd seen nothing of him afterwards. What Livia might hope to gain by it, she wasn't sure. It might be satisfaction enough to her just to plant the seeds of doubt.

'I'm not all that easily impressed,' she answered with equal smoothness.

Seemingly about to make some further comment, Lucius apparently thought better of it. Conversation moved on— as did the clock. Stifling a yawn, Gina wondered if she would ever become accustomed to the order of things. Apart from when she'd been out somewhere for the evening back home, she'd been used to going to bed around eleven at the latest.

Back home. It wasn't the first time she had felt the longing to be there. For all its grandeur, San Cotone could never mean as much to her as the house where she had been born and done her growing up. She missed so much about her life previous to the one she was leading now.

There had been times when she had felt just being with Lucius at all was enough, but it wasn't. She needed to be loved the way she loved him. She stole a glance at him as he listened to something his mother was saying, remembering the way he had looked that afternoon in the hut— the things he had done to her. If lovemaking was an art, then he was master of it, but it was no substitute for the real thing.

She caught Marcello's eye as she looked away again, surprised for a moment by the empathy she saw there. She had had so little to do with him up to now. He tended to keep himself very much to himself—in public, at any rate. They had something in common by virtue of the fact that both of them were newcomers to the Carandente clan, but his position, reliant on what he probably considered little better than charity, was a great deal harder than hers to bear.

She gave him a tentative smile, rewarded by a glimmer in return. From now on, she resolved, she would make an effort to get to know him a bit better.

For the first time since their marriage, Lucius contented himself with no more than a kiss on retiring. Quid pro quo

for her refusal earlier? Gina wondered hollowly as he settled himself for sleep.

Unlikely, she was bound to acknowledge. Lucius wasn't
a man to play that kind of game. Which left a lack of
desire as the only explanation—with Livia very much to
the forefront as the possible reason for it.

She slept eventually, coming half awake again some
time later to stretch out an instinctive arm to the warm,
male body at her side. Except that there was no body, and
hadn't been for some considerable time if the coolness of
the sheets was anything to go by.

Rolling onto her back again, Gina lay like a log, trying
not to think the worst. No matter how great the temptation,
Lucius would surely hesitate to give way to it in such a
manner. Yet he wasn't in either of the bathrooms because
no light showed beneath the doors, so where the devil *had*
he gone?

An age seemed to pass before the bedroom door was
softly opened. Gina stifled the urge to demand to know
where he'd been, controlling her breathing to appear asleep
as he slid into the bed. The silence was heavy, then she
heard a long, drawn sigh. If he'd touched her in any way
at that moment she would have been physically sick.

Awake half the night, she was late surfacing from a sleep
that had held a quality of emotional if not physical ex-
haustion. It was no surprise to find Lucius already gone.
As he'd told her that very first morning, he was an invet-
erate early riser.

She'd know nothing of this if she'd been content to
leave the past alone to start with, she thought wretchedly
as she got herself ready to go down and face the woman
she was pretty sure had seen a great deal more of her

husband than she had herself last night. Running a wife *and* mistress might be common practice for a man out here for all she knew, but in the same house was surely beyond the pale!

Breakfast was long over by the time she reached the terrace, the family dispersed. Gina drank the fresh coffee Crispina brought out to her, and nibbled a croissant without appetite. She felt listless, movement of any kind an effort. It took the sight of Lucius approaching from the lower gardens with Livia by his side to rouse her from her lethargy.

'*Buon giorno!*' greeted the other woman as they mounted the terrace steps. The derisive gleam in her eyes belied the solicitation in her voice as she added in English, 'You must have been very weary last night to sleep for so long!'

Gina took care to keep her own voice level. 'I suppose I must. I take it you've been up and about for hours!'

Livia laughed and lifted her shoulders. 'Perhaps two, no more. Even so, I found Lucius was before me.'

'Two early birds!' This time Gina couldn't quite eradicate the sarcasm, drawing a narrowed glance from Lucius. 'A big help when it comes to worm-gathering.'

It was Livia's turn to frown. 'Worm?'

Lucius answered in Italian, turning the frown to a comprehensive nod.

'So true,' she said.

Gina would have loved to know just what translation he'd given. One thing she did know: *he* was fully aware of her meaning.

'The coffee's fresh if you fancy some more,' she said.

Lucius shook his head. 'I have things I must do.'

'I will join you,' declared Livia. She turned an intimate

smile on her host. 'Perhaps you would ask Crispina to bring me out a cup?'

There was a bell connected to the table by which to summon the staff, but he didn't point it out. 'Of course,' he said.

He gave Gina a penetrating look in passing. She returned it unblinkingly. Let him wonder just how much she guessed of his night-time activities.

Livia took a seat, her whole manner proprietary. 'You must find our world very different from your own,' she remarked.

'Not all that much,' Gina responded. 'We have women like you where I come from too.'

The well-shaped brows lifted in sardonic enquiry. 'Women like me?'

'Who can't leave any man alone.'

Livia looked amused. 'It takes two of the same mind. Lucius and I have been…friends for many moons.'

'But he married *me*.'

'He was bound by a code no *Inglese* could ever understand,' came the unmoved reply.

She was half Italian, Gina could have pointed out. She didn't because it was a futile exercise.

Crispina's arrival with fresh crockery afforded her breathing space. It was unlikely that the girl would understand a word, but she waited until she had departed before voicing the declaration already formed in her mind.

'This will be your last visit to San Cotone, so make the most of what's left of it.'

All trace of derision suddenly flown, Livia looked ready to explode. 'Who are you,' she demanded, 'to tell me that?'

'Owner of everything you see, for one thing.' Gina regretted the retort the moment the words were out of her mouth, but there was no going back on them now. 'That gives me the right to say who is and who isn't welcome,' she added, thinking she may as well go the whole hog. 'So I'd be grateful if you'd pack your bag and leave as soon as possible.'

'If you think that Lucius will allow you to do this, you have little knowledge of him.' Livia spat the words at her. 'When I tell him what you have said to me—'

'You can tell him whatever you like,' Gina cut in, losing what little tolerance she had left. 'He's my husband, not my controller! If you—'

She broke off as a sudden wave of nausea gripped her by the throat. She fought to keep her face from reflecting what was going on inside her—glad of the lack of comprehension in Livia's expression.

'I'll leave you to finish your coffee,' she said, getting carefully to her feet.

Another wave of nausea made further speech impossible. She headed indoors, only just making it to a lavatory. If confirmation was needed, she thought weakly when it was over, then this had to be it. Right now, it was the last thing she wanted to think about.

Emerging from the room with the intention of going upstairs, she was dismayed to run into Cornelia. Her mother-in-law took one look at her wan face and jumped to an immediate and delighted conclusion.

'Why have you not said you were with child?' she exclaimed.

Gina attempted a smile. 'We thought we'd wait until it was official.'

'I would say there is little doubt of it. I too suffered the malaise. It only lasts the first weeks. After that, all is well.'

With the baby perhaps, Gina thought hollowly.

'You must take care not to overexert yourself,' her

mother-in-law advised. 'And you must see a physician at once!'

'Lucius is going to arrange it,' Gina assured her, anxious to escape any further catechism. 'I think I'll go and lie down for a few minutes until it passes.

'Yes, do that,' Cornelia urged. 'I am so very happy! A grandchild at last!'

'It may not be a boy,' Gina felt bound to point out, and received an expansive gesture.

'If not this time, then the next.'

Gina gave a weak smile, and made her escape. It was difficult enough dealing with the here and now.

Just how difficult was brought home to her some fifteen minutes later when Lucius came to find her. The words he was about to utter faded on his lips when he saw her lying on the bed, replaced by concerned ones.

'You are feeling ill?'

'No more than is normal, according to your mother,' she said.

'You told her?'

Sitting up now, Gina shook her head, wishing she hadn't, as nausea stirred once more. 'I didn't need to tell her. She guessed. Apparently she went through the same thing during the first few weeks. She's delighted, by the way.'

'I would hope so,' he returned. 'We are to see the gynaecologist tomorrow at eleven.'

'We?' Gina queried softly.

'You think I would allow you to go alone?' Lucius paused, expression clouding again. 'I spoke with Livia a few moments ago. She tells me you have forbidden her to visit San Cotone.'

'True.' Gina saw no point in beating about the bush.

'I'm exercising my right as mistress of the house...' she gave the term subtle emphasis '...to choose who is and isn't welcome.'

'As Ottavia's closest and dearest friend, Livia has always been welcome here.'

'As Ottavia's friend, I've no objection to her.'

A spark sprang to life deep down in the dark eyes, though his tone remained level. 'What is it you are saying?'

Gina knew a sudden flicker of doubt, but she gave it no time to grow. 'I'm saying that whatever the custom in this country, I don't have to go along with it. I gave up a whole way of life to salve your conscience, but turning a blind eye while you console yourself with old friends wasn't part of the bargain!'

The silence that followed was weighty. All expression had been wiped from Lucius's face. When he did speak it was with control. 'You believe that is what I am doing?'

'Well, isn't it?' She shot the words at him. 'Where else did you go last night if it wasn't to...her?'

'Where indeed?' The dark eyes were shuttered, the lines of his face etched in sharp relief. 'Denials would obviously be a waste of time and breath. Of course, there will be nothing to stop me from seeing Livia away from here.'

He was turning as he spoke, with the obvious intention of leaving the room. Gina's chest hurt from the pressure building within. So now she knew for sure. For what good it had done her.

'Don't you dare ever touch me again!' She flung the words after him. 'Not in any way! Do you hear me?'

The broad shoulders stiffened, but he made no answer. Gina sank back into the pillows as the door closed in his wake, misery swamping her. This time yesterday she had been so happy. Why had she had to go and spoil it all?

Because there was no way she could live with suspicion locked away inside her, came the answer. What she had to decide now was where she went from here. Home, was her immediate inclination. Her parents would welcome her with open arms.

Except that it wasn't only herself she had to consider. The child she was carrying had rights too.

The knock on the door some time later jerked her out of it. She sat up and swung her legs to the floor before inviting the knocker to enter. Cornelia regarded her in some concern.

'If you are still suffering the nausea I will have the doctor sent for,' she said.

'I'm not,' Gina assured her. 'Not any more. I must have fallen asleep.' She got to her feet, summoning a smile. 'I'll be right down.'

'There is no hurry,' her mother-in-law returned. 'Lucius said you were to be left alone, but what would a man know about such matters? He should have stayed with you to soothe your brow.' The last she said with a twinkle. 'Why should we have to bear all the crosses?'

'All part and parcel of being a woman, I suppose,' Gina answered in like vein. She made a show of examining the skirt she was wearing. 'This is all creased. I'd better change.'

'Then, I will leave you to do so,' said Cornelia. 'You will find me on the terrace should you wish for company. You knew Lucius had gone to Siena, of course?'

'Of course,' Gina echoed, doubting if it was true. He would be with Livia.

Knowing Lucius's opinion of the garment, she more often than not refrained from wearing trousers of any kind. Today, she donned a pair of loose silky ones in place of the skirt. No more kowtowing to his likes and dislikes. From now on she pleased herself.

A furious Ottavia cornered her on her way downstairs.

'I grew tired of waiting for you to appear!' she declared. 'How dare you tell Livia she cannot come here again!'

'How dare *you* tell *me* what I should or shouldn't do?' Gina countered, losing what self-possession she had managed to gather in face of this fresh attack. 'I'll make whatever decision I choose to make. If you object, you can always find somewhere else to live!'

The fury died as swiftly as it had arisen before the look on her sister-in-law's face. She knew instant shame that she could have stooped so low. 'I didn't mean that,' she said gruffly. 'I really didn't!'

'Why would you say it unless it was in your mind?' Ottavia retorted. 'I have known from the beginning that you resented both my own and Marcello's presence. No doubt you would prefer that my mother was also gone!'

'Not true.' Gina searched her mind for some way of undoing the harm she had done—finding nothing of any great help. 'The only one whose presence I resent is Livia Marucchi,' she appealed. 'You can surely understand that?'

Ottavia curled a lip. 'I understand your jealousy of her beauty, but banning her from San Cotone will not make Lucius more attentive towards you. My brother did what he considered his duty in marrying you. Why should he sacrifice everything?'

'He had the opportunity to marry Livia before ever I came along,' Gina responded, trying to keep a level head. 'Why didn't he take it, I wonder?'

'Because Livia herself was not yet ready to make the commitment.'

'I don't believe that.'

The shrug was expressive. 'You must believe what comforts you. I shall, of course, be telling Lucius of your wish for Marcello and myself to find other accommodation.'

Hopeless trying any further appeal, Gina accepted despondently as the older woman turned away. It would normally be against her nature to say what she had, but what about this whole situation was normal? She was married to and carrying the child of a man who not only didn't love her, but was at present very probably in the arms of the woman he had wanted to marry.

She avoided contact with any other member of the family by returning to the bedroom. The nausea had passed, for what difference it made to her mood. Lying on the bed, she went over the happenings of the last weeks. There had been good times—wonderful times, in fact—but how real had they been? How often when making love to her had Lucius imagined she was Livia? How often had he compared her responses with those of the other woman?

How did she go on living this life knowing what she knew?

CHAPTER TEN

SHE must have dozed off at some point, waking with a start to find Donata standing by the bedside.

'I was concerned when you made no answer to my knock,' said the girl. 'Are you still feeling ill?'

Gina raised herself up, forcing a smile. 'Not any more, thanks.' She glanced at the bedside clock, dismayed to find it approaching twelve-thirty. 'I can't believe it!' she exclaimed. 'Where did the time go?'

'You need whatever rest your body tells you you need now,' declared Donata with some authority. '*Madre* says she slept a great deal when she was with child.'

Gina's head jerked round. 'She told you!'

'But of course.' Donata looked momentarily nonplussed. 'Was she not meant to?'

'No. I mean, it hasn't been properly confirmed yet.'

'But you know yourself?'

'Well…yes.' Gina summoned another smile, a lighter note. 'I suppose I'm being overcautious.'

Dark eyes sparkled. 'It's so exciting! Lucius must be joyful!' She sobered to add sternly, 'He should have stayed with you while you were feeling ill.'

'I'm best dealing with it on my own.' Gina kept her tone easy.

'Do you wish me to leave you?' queried her sister-in-law with obvious reluctance.

'Not at all,' Gina assured her. 'You can find me something uncreased to wear to lunch while I take a quick

168

shower to freshen up, if you like, then we'll go down together.'

Her multireflection in the bathroom was no confidence booster. She looked thoroughly washed out, her hair limp and lifeless. It was far too early yet, of course, to detect any change in her slender shape, but it was going to come. Whether she would still be here at San Cotone when the child came into the world was another matter.

Donata had picked out a sleeveless tunic in muted greens, along with a pair of low-heeled sandals.

'High heels are no longer suitable,' she advised. 'You must take no risks with your balance.' She eyed Gina's figure in the brief lace bra and panties. 'You'll need maternal clothing for when you begin to gain weight.'

'Maternity,' Gina corrected, unable to stay sombre in the face of such knowledgeable pronouncements. 'Maternal means mother.'

'Which is what you're to be.' Donata sounded as if the distinction was too slight to be of any great importance. 'And *I* am to be an aunt! Practice,' she added, 'for when I have children of my own.'

'You plan on Cesare becoming the father?' Gina asked, sliding the tunic over her head.

'Of course.' There was certainty in both voice and expression. 'He knows it too, even if the words themselves are still to be spoken between us.'

Recalling what he'd said yesterday, Gina felt it quite possible. She only hoped Donata wouldn't suffer the same disillusionment she was suffering in time to come.

Not looking forward to seeing Ottavia again, she was relieved, if only temporarily, to find Cornelia seated alone on the terrace.

'You look far from your usual self,' remarked the latter

candidly, viewing her. 'Would you not prefer to have a tray brought to you?'

'I'm fine now,' Gina assured her. 'Really I am. I was just a bit tired, that's all.'

'You perhaps have need of an iron supplement.'

'If I do, I'm sure it will all be sorted out tomorrow when I see the gynaecologist.' Gina sought a change of subject. 'The air feels heavy again. Do you think we're in for another storm?'

'There is a likelihood at this time of the year.' Cornelia sounded amused. 'It must be your English blood that makes you so concerned with the weather.'

Gina laughed. 'It's so rarely the same from one day to another back home!'

The older woman looked at her oddly. 'You still think of England as your home?'

She was saved from answering by Ottavia's emergence from the villa, closely followed by Lucius. There was little to be gleaned from his expression, but Gina had no doubt at all that he'd been fully apprised of her transgressions.

'Business concluded?' she heard herself asking.

'Whatever is left will be dealt with another time,' he returned without particular inflection. 'How are you feeling now?'

She stretched her lips in a smile she hoped didn't look as stiff as it felt. 'I'll live.'

Ottavia looked from one to the other in some obvious perplexity. It was left to her mother to put her in the picture.

'Did Lucius not tell you yet? You are to be a *zietta*!'

The expression in Ottavia's eyes was hardly one of pleasure at the news. 'You must forgive me,' she said with satire to Gina, 'for my failure to appreciate your condition earlier. My attention was on other matters.'

'I already told you I didn't mean what I said,' Gina responded on as steady a note as she could manage. 'I apologise for it.'

'Once said, such things cannot be easily forgotten,' came the brittle reply.

'But they can be put aside,' said Lucius crisply. 'Gina has apologised. Let that be an end to it.'

Ottavia lifted her shoulders in a gesture meant to express a reluctant acquiescence. Bursting though they obviously were with curiosity, neither Cornelia nor Donata voiced a question. Meeting her husband's hard eyes, Gina did her best to keep the desolation she felt from showing in hers. No way was he ever going to know her true feelings.

Reluctant to face the questions she was sure Donata for one would be asking, she escaped into the gardens after lunch. There was to be no escape from Lucius however. He found her down by the lily pond where they had met that first morning.

'There are matters we have to have clear between us,' he said.

Gina kept her gaze fixed on the dragonfly flitting from lily pad to lily pad. 'They're clear enough already. Unlike with Ottavia, I meant what I told *you* this morning. I don't want you anywhere near me again!'

'You expect me to accept such an edict?'

He had halted to the side and a little behind the stone seat where she was sitting, right on the periphery of her vision. Her heart was hammering so loudly he must have been able to hear it, but her voice was rock steady. 'You don't have a choice.'

'As your husband, I have certain rights!'

Her head jerked round, eyes blazing into his. 'Like hell

you do! I'm not your property to be used as and when you see fit!'

Dark eyes glittered back at her, the thrust of his hands into trouser pockets indicative of a barely controlled anger. 'I recall no complaints.'

'*I've* no basis for comparison,' she retorted. 'Yet.'

The glitter became a flame, searing her where she sat. He reached her in a couple of steps, jerking her upright. 'There will be no other man in your life!' he said in a clipped voice. 'Should you ever…'

A muscle in his jaw line contracted as his teeth came together. He released her abruptly, striding away without a backward glance. Gina sank back to her seat. She couldn't continue with this, she thought bleakly.

There was no sign of Lucius when she eventually forced herself to return to the villa. Neither was Ottavia nor her mother in evidence. Which left only Donata.

'I saw Lucius follow you to the gardens, and again when he returned,' the girl declared. 'He was angrier than I have seen him since I was sent home from school!'

'We had a disagreement,' Gina acknowledged.

It was apparent that her sister-in-law wanted to ask about what, but she refrained. 'Unlike Ottavia's, his anger doesn't last long,' she advised. 'He will have forgotten it when he returns.'

Not in this instance, reflected Gina hollowly.

Hot and sultry, the afternoon crept to a close. It needed another storm to bring relief. Lucius, it turned out, had gone to the vineyard. He returned with Marcello at six, seemingly bearing out Donata's prediction. Surface only, Gina judged, wondering if she was the only one to see the fiery flicker in the dark eyes whenever he glanced her way.

Taking it for granted that Ottavia would have filled him in on the day's happenings, she sought a few minutes with Marcello before going to change for dinner.

'I was in a bad mood this morning and let my tongue run away with me,' she said frankly. 'I'd hate for you to think I didn't want you here.'

His smile was wry. 'It would be understandable.'

'It's not the way I really feel,' Gina insisted. About you, at any rate, she tagged on mentally. 'San Cotone is as much your home as it is mine.'

'That can never be,' he returned. 'I am deeply indebted to Lucius for providing a roof over my head, but the time must come when I seek a home of my own again.'

The problem being that Ottavia was unlikely to settle for what she would regard as an impoverished standard of living, Gina reflected, feeling genuine sympathy for the man.

'Please try to excuse my wife if she appears resentful of you,' he went on. 'The realisation of who you were was a devastation to her.'

If Ottavia hadn't searched her things that day, in all likelihood there would have been no realisation, Gina could have told him.

'I suppose I can appreciate her feelings,' she said instead. 'Especially considering...'

'Considering my position,' Marcello finished for her as she let the words trail away. 'You must wonder that we are together still.'

'It's crossed my mind,' she admitted.

'As with most who have little knowledge of her. Her loyalty to me is steadfast. Never once has she berated me for my mistakes. To Ottavia, the marriage vows are sacred.'

Providing she wasn't called on to suffer the 'poorer' element, came the sneaking thought.

'You must love her a great deal,' she murmured.

'A very great deal,' he confirmed. 'She is everything to me.'

Gina had never envied anyone in her life before, but she felt a pang right now. One thing she could be certain of, Lucius was never going to say the same of her.

He was already in the shower when she went up. Reluctant to be drawn into any further altercations, she lingered as long as possible under the water herself, hoping he would have gone by the time she emerged. Finding her hope granted when she did eventually regain the bedroom brought only a temporary relief, of course. She had to be alone with him again at some point; while they still shared a bed, she could hardly avoid it. Just let him try exercising the rights he had claimed this afternoon, she thought fiercely, and the whole house would know about it!

It was a long evening, made even longer by Ottavia's unabated hostility. Apart from not having a great deal to say, Lucius gave no indication that anything was amiss. Gina put on a show herself, but was aware of Cornelia's thoughtful regard from time to time.

Donata was too wrapped up in her own affairs to sense any discord. 'Tomorrow,' she announced at dinner, 'Cesare is to take me to Firenze to meet with his grandmother. She will disapprove of me, of course, but I will win her over.'

Gina didn't doubt it. Shorn of the rebel outlook she had first displayed, her sister-in-law was capable of winning anyone over. She had certainly succeeded with Cesare, for all his protestations.

By midnight she had had enough. Cornelia nodded sagely when she announced her intention of going to bed.

'You must learn to take siesta,' she said. 'Rest is good for you.'

'I'll be with you shortly,' said Lucius. His tone was devoid of any undercurrents, but to Gina it still sounded like a threat.

She prepared for bed swiftly, sliding between the cool silk sheets to lie wide awake and tense. Only when the outer door finally opened did she close her eyes, turning her face into the pillow and deepening her breathing.

Every sound, every movement Lucius made over the following minutes seemed magnified. When he got into the bed, she could barely restrain the tremoring in her limbs.

'We must talk,' he said.

Gina gave up on the pretence. 'There's nothing left to say. If it weren't for the baby, I'd be out of here by now!'

He drew in a harsh breath. 'This has gone far enough! What proof do you have of your accusations?'

'Proof?' She rolled onto her back to direct a blazing gaze. 'You admitted it!'

Supported on an elbow, Lucius regarded her with held-in anger. 'I admitted nothing!'

'You didn't deny it.'

'You would have believed me if I had?'

She hesitated, searching his taut, olive-skinned features for some assurance—finding none because the dark eyes gave so little away. 'If you weren't with Livia last night,' she said at length, 'then where were you?'

His expression underwent an indefinable alteration. 'I was walking the gardens.'

'For two hours or more?'

'If that was how long I was gone, then yes.'

'You really expect me to believe *that*!'

The moments stretched interminably as he studied her, the muscles around his mouth showing white beneath his skin from the pressure applied. When he spoke at last it was with iron control. 'If you doubt it still, then you were right. There *is* nothing left to say.'

Gina lay like a stone as he switched out the bedside light and settled himself for sleep, his turned back a barrier. Even if she disregarded what Mario Lanciani had told her yesterday, Ottavia had made the situation clear enough this morning, she defended herself. What else could she believe?

Scarcely needed, the confirmation that she was indeed pregnant brought little immediate cheer. Driving back from Siena with a silent Lucius at the wheel, Gina contemplated a future devoid of even physical closeness, much less love.

She stole a glance at the finely carved profile outlined against a sky still heavy with cloud, wondering what was really going on inside the proud dark head. Even if she could extract a promise from him not to see Livia again, could she trust him to keep it?

'I have business in Rome tomorrow,' he said shortly. 'I must leave this afternoon.'

Gina made no answer, her despondency reaching new depths. Lucius tautened his jaw.

'I hope to find you in a more receptive frame of mind on my return.'

'Receptive to what?' she asked. 'More lies?'

This time it was Lucius who made no answer, knuckles paling as he gripped the wheel. Gina felt suddenly sick. As he had said last night, what actual proof did she have of his involvement with Livia Marucchi? The word of a man she'd never met before yesterday? Of a woman who hated her? Not so much the actual word in the latter case even. Ottavia had only insinuated.

'I'm sorry,' she said thickly. 'I think I might be on the way to paranoia!'

Lucius was a moment or two responding, his profile still austere. 'Are you saying you believe what I tell you after all?'

She made a wry gesture, turning a deaf ear to the misgivings still hovering at the back of her mind. 'Yes.'

He said no more on the subject, but the atmosphere remained heavy. Gina put her head back against the seat rest and closed her eyes. She felt so utterly dispirited.

Lucius left for Rome immediately after lunch. Gina saw him off, aware when he kissed her goodbye of constraint in his embrace. Telling him she believed him innocent of any double-dealing was only half the battle she had with herself, she acknowledged wearily. To do the job properly, she had to reinstate Livia's visiting privileges. That was going to be one of the hardest things she had ever done.

At Cornelia's urging, she retired to the bedroom for siesta, but found little rest. It was no use putting off the evil moment until tomorrow, she decided in the end. If it was going to be done at all, it had to be now.

There was only one Marucchi listed in the telephone book. She dialled the number, struggling against the urge to abandon the whole idea. The call was answered by a man whose manner indicated a member of the family rather than a servant. Gina asked in Italian to speak with Signorina Marucchi, but was forced to request a translation of the fast-spoken response.

She sat for several moments fighting a new inner battle after replacing the receiver—without success. It was too much of a coincidence that Livia should be away from

home for a few days at the very same time as Lucius. If
Rome was his destination, then it was hers too without
doubt.

Like an automaton, she got up and made for the dressing
room, selecting a lightweight skirt and jacket from the
wardrobe and putting them on, then sliding her feet into a
pair of shoes. With no suitcase to hand, she could take
little with her, but she was going regardless. Home to
England where she belonged. Back to those whose love
she could count on.

Her face looked pale in the mirror, her eyes bruised. She
closed her mind to everything other than the here and now,
considering her options for getting away. Keys for all the
cars in the garages were looked after by the man who
tended the vehicles. All she had to do was request one.
From Florence, she could fly home.

She made it to the garages without running into anyone
at all, to find the off-shot room, where the keys were kept,
unattended. Gina unhooked a set from the numbered pegs
at random, only realising she had chosen the Ferarri when
she reached the appropriate stall. She'd driven it only the
once, and then with Lucius along, but she didn't hesitate.
It would get her where she wanted to go.

Converted from stables, the garaging block had an in-
dividual door for every car. It slid open on oiled runners.
There was plenty of fuel she saw on switching on the ig-
nition. More than enough to get her to Florence.

The engine started at the first pull. Gina bit her lip at
the powerful sound, expecting it to bring immediate attention. Not that it was anyone's business but her own if she
chose to take the vehicle out.

A couple of the groundsmen were the only people to
see her leave. She reached the Vernici road without mishap, turning north away from the town to head for the

highway that would take her to Florence. It seemed more like years than mere months since she had traversed these same roads on the way here, she thought bleakly. If only she'd never bothered!

The rain started when she had gone barely five kilometres, so heavy the windscreen wipers could barely cope. She should stop and wait it out, Gina knew, but that would give her too much time to think about what she was doing. She didn't want to think about anything other than getting away.

The truck looming suddenly through the murk was right on the crown of the road. A sense of *déjà vu* swept over her as she took instinctive avoiding action. There was a timeless moment when the car skidded out of control as the tyres failed to grip, then a huge bang, and darkness.

She drifted up from the depths to the sound of voices, faint and far away at first, but becoming stronger. They were speaking in Italian, of course, and far too rapidly for her to follow. *'Non capisco,'* she murmured before drifting off again.

Her first clear recollection found her lying on her back with a white ceiling filling her line of vision. Her neck felt stiff. She lifted a nerveless hand to touch the collar encircling it, the pieces coming together slowly. Apart from the headache throbbing at her temples, there was no pain.

'You must lie still until they can be sure there is no further damage,' said Lucius from somewhere off to the side.

The anguish that swept her was like a sword thrust. 'The baby.' she whispered. 'I lost the baby?'

'No.' Lucius came into view, the strain evident in both face and voice. 'You still have the child. The seat belt saved you from being thrown around the car when it rolled.'

'Is it a write-off?' she murmured. 'The car, I mean.'

'You think I care about the car?' he demanded with force. 'Why were you driving at all in such weather?'

Gina gazed at the ceiling, in no fit state for the confrontation that would eventually have to come. 'It wasn't raining when I set off.'

'That is not—' Lucius broke off abruptly. When he spoke again it was on a more level note. 'You were drifting in and out of consciousness for several hours. That means you have concussion at the very least. The doctor will examine you now you're fully awake.'

He moved away, his place taken by an older man in a white coat. Gina submitted to his ministrations, responding to the questions translated for her by Lucius. Her relief at the removal of the neck collar, indicating that there was no spinal injury, was tempered by the headache still pounding at her temples. She sat up gingerly when asked, wincing a little as pressure came to bear on bruises she hadn't felt until then, but thankful to have no greater injuries to cope with.

The two men spoke together for a few moments, then the doctor left.

'You're to stay here at least for tonight to make sure there are no delayed repercussions,' Lucius declared. 'Sleep is the best medicine for you. A nurse will be in shortly to make you comfortable.'

'Where *is* here?' Gina asked, more because she felt it expected of her than through any great desire to know.

'The Emanuele Clinic. The accident happened less than a kilometre away.'

'You were on your way to Rome,' she said.

'I naturally turned back on receiving the news.' Tone

steady, eyes impenetrable, he added, '*Madre* was distraught. She was unaware of your departure from the villa at all. Where were you going?'

This was neither the time nor the place for confrontation, Gina acknowledged wearily. 'I just felt like a drive,' she said. 'I'm sorry to have given your mother concern.'

Fire flashed in the dark depths. 'You think her the only one to be concerned? If you could but—' He broke off once again, shaking his head as if in repudiation of what he'd been about to say, face set. 'Tomorrow will be time enough. You have need of sleep.'

Gina reached out an involuntary hand to grasp the bare, bronzed forearm as he began turning away, unable to hold out any longer against the emotions choking her.

'Don't go,' she said huskily. 'I need you, *mi amore*!'

His jaw contracted, the muscles in the arm she held taut beneath the skin. 'Do not use that term without true meaning!'

'I don't.' Gina was past caring about giving herself away. Her voice gathered strength along with her spirit. 'I know you don't feel as deeply for me as I feel for you, but you'd better start learning because I'm not letting go! I'll give any woman who fancies her chances with you a battle royal!'

It was a moment or two before Lucius responded, the expression dawning in his eyes as he gazed at her increasing her already galloping pulse rate to ungovernable proportions.

'From where,' he said at last, 'did you gather the impression that I had no depth of feeling for you?'

Gina lifted her shoulders uncertainly. 'You've never used the word love.'

The faintest of smiles touched his mouth. 'Would words of love have persuaded you to marry me?'

'It would have helped.'

'I doubt it. You were drawn to me physically, but no more than that.'

Gina searched the handsome face. 'You're saying the marriage wasn't *just* a matter of conscience on your part?'

His smile widened a little. 'I fell in love with the girl who gave herself so unreservedly to me that night. The girl I had every intention of making my wife, both before and after I discovered her true identity. Reprehensible of me though it was to take advantage of your father's financial problems, I saw no other means of persuading you.'

He took one of her hands in his, raising it to his lips. 'My love for you knows no limits, *mi tesoro*. You must believe me when I tell you that Livia Marucchi has never, nor ever could, hold a place in my heart. I was angry when you banned her from visiting San Cotone again, yes, but only because you accepted my guilt without question. I walked in the gardens two nights ago in an agony of mind, believing you would never come to love me the way I yearned for you to love me. To have you accuse me of spending those hours with Livia—'

'I was too eaten up with jealousy to see straight,' Gina cut in wryly. 'She's so beautiful!'

'Her beauty bears no comparison with yours!' Lucius declared. 'To look into her eyes is to look into soulless depths! A man may use a woman of her kind for release, but few could countenance any closer relationship.'

'Might you not find a need for that kind of release in future?' Gina murmured, and saw the dark eyes flare again.

'You still think me so devoid of integrity?'

'Love doesn't automatically instil total trust,' she defended. 'You've been used to a full and free sex life. Is one woman going to be enough for you?'

Lucius let go of her hand to place both of his about her

throat, lifting her face to meet his descending mouth. The tenderness in his kiss was more convincing than any words.

'*This* one woman, yes,' he avowed when he lifted his head again. 'You satisfy every craving in me—and always will.'

He released her with reluctance. 'Enough for now. You must rest. I'll return in the morning to—'

'No!' Gina ignored the ache in her head as she shook it emphatically. 'I'm coming home with you now!'

'The doctor said—' he began.

'I don't care what the doctor said! You can keep an eye on me yourself. If you try leaving me here I'll walk out and thumb a lift!' she threatened as he hesitated. 'I mean it, Lucius!'

'I knew you were going to be a trouble to me the first moment I saw you,' he remarked with humour. 'What I failed to foresee was the extent of it. If I removed your clothing from the wardrobe you would have no choice but to stay.'

'Don't count on it. I'd wrap myself in a sheet if necessary!'

Laughter creased the sculptured face. 'A risk I am not prepared to take! Do you feel capable of dressing yourself while I go and speak with the doctor?'

'Perfectly,' she assured him. 'I'll be ready and waiting.'

He kissed her again, long and passionately, before departing, leaving her with a brimming heart. She could deal with anything and anyone knowing he loved her—including Ottavia. San Cotone was her home, as it had been her father's before her. She finally felt she belonged.

EPILOGUE

EXTENDED along the length of the terrace to seat the laughing, chattering throng, the table groaned beneath the weight of dishes still nowhere near empty. Crystal and silver glinted in the sunlight, while myriad scents spilled from the massed blooms festooning the stone balustrades.

Gina turned her gaze from the distant views she never tired of to the infinitely dearer one closer to hand, tears of pure happiness prickling her lids as she surveyed each familiar face. It was wonderful to have everyone together like this: an occasion to be cherished in memory for all time. And all down to her mother-in-law, who had moved heaven and earth to make it happen.

Catching the latter's eye, she mouthed her gratitude, finishing off with a blown kiss, and receiving one in return. This meant so much more to her than any formal celebration, as Cornelia had known it would.

Secure in the knowledge of their own status in her affections, her parents watched the exchange without rancour. They were regular visitors to San Cotone, and would be welcomed as permanent residents if and when they finally chose. As Lucius himself often said, there was room enough and to spare.

Even more so these days, came the thought, bringing a momentary downswing in spirits, just as swiftly conquered. She had flown the coop herself at an earlier age than either Vittorio or Giovanni. Anyway, Doria was still within easy reach, and soon to give birth to a brother or sister for Pietro and Portia. They helped make up for the lack of day-to-day contact with the other grandchildren.

Sitting here now, it still scarcely seemed possible that so much time had passed. The silver in Lucius's hair served only to enhance the sculptured bone structure, the fine cotton T-shirt he was wearing outlining a body still as lean and lithe as when they had first met. Husband and lover without equal, Gina thought mistily, senses stirring as always to the sheer impact of those looks. There would never come a time when she failed to want him, never come a time when her love for him burned any less intense.

Her whole life here in Tuscany had been a joy. Not once had she known regret for the career she had given up to become a wife and mother. She and Ottavia had long ago reached an understanding—helped by Marcello's regaining of independence—and were now the best of friends. The two remained childless themselves, but took great delight in all their nieces and nephews. Donata and Cesare were the proud parents of no less than five children, all of whom were here today too, along with their respective families, making a grand total of thirty-eight. What might be called a typical Italian family gathering.

Lucius was getting to his feet, clinking a spoon against his glass to draw attention.

'I wish to propose a toast of my own,' he said. He looked down at the lovely, unlined face at his side, dark eyes filled with an emotion that brought a lump to Gina's throat. 'To my beautiful, incomparable wife, for twenty-five wonderful years! And for all those yet to come!'

The world's bestselling romance series.

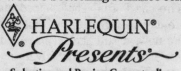

Seduction and Passion Guaranteed!

They're the men who have everything— except a bride...

Wealth, power, charm—what else could a heart-stopping handsome tycoon need? Find out in the GREEK TYCOONS miniseries, where your very favorite authors introduce gorgeous Greek multimillionaires who are in need of wives!

Coming soon in Harlequin Presents®

SMOKESCREEN MARRIAGE by Sara Craven
#2320, on sale May 2003

THE GREEK TYCOON'S BRIDE by Helen Brooks
#2328, on sale June 2003

THE GREEK'S SECRET PASSION by Sharon Kendrick
#2339, on sale August 2003

Available wherever Harlequin books are sold.

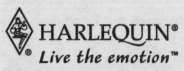

Visit us at www.eHarlequin.com

HPGTYC

The world's bestselling romance series.

HARLEQUIN®
Presents

Seduction and Passion Guaranteed!

Anything can happen behind closed doors!

Do you dare find out...?

Meet Crystal and Sam, a couple thrown together by circumstances into a whirlwind of unexpected attraction. Forced into each other's company whether they like it or not, they're soon in the grip of passion—and definitely *don't* want to be disturbed!

Popular Harlequin Presents® author Carole Mortimer explores this delicious fantasy in a tantalizing romance you simply won't want to put down.

AN ENIGMATIC MAN

#2316

April on-sale

Available wherever Harlequin books are sold.

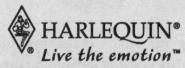

HARLEQUIN®
Live the emotion™

Visit us at www.eHarlequin.com

HPDNDIS

Available in March from *USA TODAY* bestselling author

LINDSAY McKENNA

A brand-new book in her bestselling series

MORGAN'S MERCENARIES: DESTINY'S WOMEN

AN
HONORABLE
WOMAN

From the moment Commanding Officer Cam Anderson met Officer Gus Morales, she knew she was in trouble. The men under Gus's command weren't used to taking orders from a woman, and Cam wasn't used to the paralyzing attraction she felt for Gus. The ruggedly handsome soldier made her feel things a commander shouldn't feel. Made her long for things no honorable woman should want....

"When it comes to action and romance, nobody does it better than Ms. McKenna."
—*Romantic Times*

Available at your favorite retail outlet.

Where love comes alive™

A "Mother of the Year" contest brings
overwhelming response as thousands of women
vie for the luxurious grand prize....

Kate Hoffmann

Jacqueline Diamond

Jill Shalvis

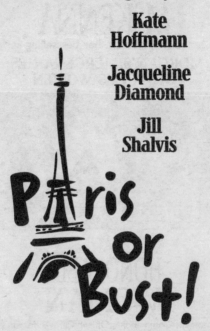

Paris or Bust!

A hilarious and romantic trio of new stories!

With a trip to Paris at stake, these women are
determined to win! But the laughs are many as three of
them discover that being finalists isn't the most
excitement they'll ever have.... Falling in love is!

Available in April 2003.

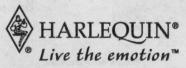